The Lost Miracle

Warning: Contents of this book can be addictive in nature. Readers may get hooked on the book and find it difficult to stop reading. Reader discretion is advised.

The Lost Miracle

Tony Agha

MythShack Publishing
2014

Disclaimer: This book is a work of fiction. Names, characters, personalities, places, incidents, and events mentioned in the book are used fictitiously and are not to be considered real. Any resemblance to actual events, locales, organizations, countries, or persons living or dead is purely coincidental

Copyright © 2014 by Agha Ahmar Ali

All rights reserved. This book or any portion thereof may not be reproduced or used in any manner whatsoever without the express written permission of the publisher except for the use of brief quotations in a book review or scholarly journal.

First Printing: 2014

ISBN 978-0-9938656-0-2

MythShack Publishing
Oakville, ON, Canada

www.MythShack.com

Cover Design by R.Atanassova@Elementi Studio Ltd.

Ordering Information:

Special discounts are available on quantity purchases by corporations, associations, educators, and others. For details, contact the publisher at: info@MythShack.com

Trade bookstores and wholesalers please contact MythShack Publishing via email: Sales@MythShack.com.

Dedication

To my lovely family.

Thank you. Without your support and patience, I would never have achieved my dream.

Contents

Acknowledgements 4
Prologue 5
Chapter 1 8
Chapter 2 16
Chapter 3 25
Chapter 4 35
Chapter 5 44
Chapter 6 51
Chapter 7 61
Chapter 8 71
Chapter 9 81
Chapter 10 91
Chapter 11 99
Chapter 12 105
Chapter 13 111
Chapter 14 121
Epilogue 134
References 137

Acknowledgements

I would like to thank my editor, my proofreader, my creative team, my book cover designers, my critic Anthony Lorraway, my tax consultants, and above all my family, without whose help this book would never have been completed.

Tony Agha

Prologue

January 1
Muskoka, ON, Canada

The meteorologists were calling it one of the most severe winters in over forty years. Icy rain over the last couple of days had made the whole town look like a fairytale land. Despite the extreme cold, Robert Stiavnicky, a middle-aged man with long, unkempt gray hair and a thin, lanky structure, was perspiring. He was sweating, not because of the heat generated by the fireplace in his hideout in the country cottage, but from the fear of losing his miraculous discovery. Unworthy people wanted to take it — people who were trying to use it for their personal benefit and who would not let the common people take advantage of this amazing find.

Rob recalled his efforts during the past week to ensure that his discovery would get to those who deserved it and felt a sigh of relief. He had traveled across the globe and hidden the clues to prevent the unworthy from uncovering them. Soon, he would have to sacrifice his life to make those pitiful individuals believe that the miracle has been lost with him. But before that, he had one final task to complete.

He pulled out his tablet from his briefcase, intending to type an encrypted message detailing the missing links to the clues he had spread across the globe. It would be addressed to the only man he could trust with his miraculous discovery. But before he could write anything, he heard a loud knock on the door.

The person outside said loudly:

"I know you're in there, Rob." The intruder banged on the door again, and threatened, "If you don't open the door in one minute, we'll break it."

Rob did not have enough time to complete his last message. He looked upward and prayed to God that the clues he had left behind would be good enough. He quickly executed a command on his tablet to erase all content. Then he threw the electronic gadget into the fireplace, so they couldn't retrieve the data. At that moment, the door slammed open, and three intruders barged in, bringing with them a gush of cold air.

Robert knew it was time to say farewell to this world. Before the intruders could say anything, he looked into the eyes of his adversary and gave him a smile. It was a smile his enemy would never forget. As he smiled, he swallowed the cyanide powder that he had recently acquired for this very moment.

The intruders tried to revive Rob, but it was too late.

*****

Chapter 1

November 25 9:00 AM (EST)
Montvale, NJ, USA

Sarah Mason had returned home last night from a few months of extensive travel, visiting art galleries along the east coast of North America as part of the planning for her next series of exhibitions there. Even though Sarah was a relatively new face in the art world, her talent had taken her to great heights. Her creative masterpieces were highly appreciated by critics and art lovers around the world.

Being a fitness freak, Sarah made it a point to spend at least an hour in the gym five days a week, even when traveling. This morning, she was dressed in a loose black t-shirt and grey gym pants under her long, white winter jacket.

Though Sarah was a simple girl and did not like wearing heavy makeup and expensive dresses, she looked beautiful in all clothes. Her conservative appearance failed to hide the beauty of her deep, innocent blue eyes and attractive figure. She had dark brown hair with light curls that were accentuated with ash-brown highlights.

After that morning's satisfying workout, she was craving a home-cooked breakfast. Sarah parked her car in the elaborate four-car garage of her beautiful colonial home and walked toward the kitchen. She hoped that her mother had prepared her favorite: mouth-watering crepes stuffed with cheese and covered with a divine white sauce, with freshly cut fruit and rye toast on the side.

Amanda, Sarah's mother, was gorgeous even at the age of sixty-five, and Sarah had clearly inherited her good looks. Upon entering the living room, Sarah dumped her coat on the couch. Smelling the divine aroma coming from the kitchen, she walked toward her mother and said:

"Mom, I'm home and super hungry." Hugging her mother from behind, she continued, "I can't resist the aroma of your crepes. Are they ready yet?"

Looking back at Sarah, Amanda said, "You're all sweaty. Why don't you take a shower first? I need ten more minutes."

Sarah crashed on her favorite rocking chair next to the large window overlooking the ravine in the backyard. She enjoyed having breakfast in this particular spot, as she could enjoy her mother's cooking and the beautiful scenery overlooking her backyard at the same time.

Sarah replied to her mother. "No, mom, I am too tired to take a shower right now. I'll do it after I eat."

While waiting, Sarah decided to pick up her phone and check her messages. As she was glancing through them, an email caught her attention. Her eyes widened as she read it. She dropped the phone on the table and ran frantically up the stairs.

Her mother was setting the breakfast table. Surprised by Sarah's behavior and not noticing the anguish on her face, she shouted:

"A minute back you couldn't move a finger, and now when the crepes are ready, you run away without eating them?" She added, "The crepes will get cold. Are you listening to me?"

Amanda didn't get a response, and that made her even more upset. She was going to give Sarah a piece of her mind when she got back.

Sarah returned after thirty minutes with a suitcase and told her mother:

"Mom, I don't have time to explain. I have to fly to Dubai; my flight is in three hours."

Amanda found it hard to digest this piece of information. Sarah was claustrophobic and always avoided air travel. She said, "What do you mean you're going to Dubai?"

Sarah looked into her mother's eyes and said, "Mother, I have to go right now; please don't ask me for details. I don't know them myself." She paused for a few seconds and added, "I promise I'll be fine. Trust me."

Amanda was left with no choice but to have faith in Sarah's judgment. Giving up on arguments, she said, "At least finish your breakfast. I know you don't eat much while traveling."

Sarah stuffed her mouth with the crepe as fast as she could and ran out the door. She jumped into a taxi that was waiting in front of the wraparound porch of their gorgeous colonial home.

Amanda was unable to figure out what could have convinced Sarah to go, alone, on this long-haul flight to Dubai. Last year, when Sarah had been invited to attend an event at the Toronto Art Gallery in her honor, she had refused to take a plane and had driven all the way instead.

Seeing her only daughter leave in such an abrupt manner on a fourteen-hour-long air trip, she couldn't get one question out of her mind: "Why?"

*****

The Lost Miracle

November 25 8:00 AM (CST)
Dallas, TX, USA

Jennifer Riggs was running late for her lecture on 'Advancement in archeological research over the last five decades' at the University of Dallas, Irving, TX. She had been invited to speak here by her longtime acquaintance, John Frazer. Frazer was an adamant fan of her research in the field of archeology and of the articles that Jennifer had written over the last five years.

To avoid further delays, Jennifer had called the bell desk from her room to arrange for a cab as she finished doing her hair. The cab was already waiting for her when she reached the main lobby of the Fairmont Hotel in downtown Dallas.

"Irving, please, and fast," Jennifer ordered the cab driver.

"Where in Irving?" asked the driver.

"University of Dallas," she blurted out coldly, to avoid any further conversation.

The cab driver, unable to take the hint, asked, "Are you a student there?" He added, "I assume in the faculty of fashion?"

Jennifer, clearly not in the mood and being a sarcastic person by nature, said, "No, I am going there for the shopping." After pausing for a second, she added, "Now, if you are done with your interview, can we please move?"

The cab driver didn't take her sarcasm well, and his frown was visible on his forehead. He was not the only one to have been deceived by her looks.

Jennifer was quite a stunner. She looked more like a model out of a fashion magazine than a historian or an archeologist. She had a commendable dress sense, and often people wondered how she managed to look so good even on archeological expeditions. Often, her female counterparts asked her how she kept her hair and clothes in perfect order even under extreme conditions.

The cabbie's driving style was not helping Jennifer's mood. After the embarrassing start, he had decided to call someone on the phone and was now paying more attention to his call than to the road.

Trying to warn the guy, Jennifer said, "Excuse me, can you please put the phone down? I don't feel safe with you driving and talking at the same time."

Her warnings went unnoticed, as the guy was busy with his conversation. She raised her voice and gave

The Lost Miracle

him a final warning, this time with clear touch of anger in her tone. "If you don't put the phone down this very second, I will report you to the authorities."

The driver looked back in his rearview mirror with a blank expression and put his call to an end. She didn't get the apology that she was expecting, and it was difficult to judge by his expression if he was sorry or amused by his act.

To get her mind off this unpleasant character, Jennifer decided to check her Facebook page using her smartphone. She had two missed calls from the university professor, who was probably trying to confirm whether Jennifer would arrive in time for her lecture. She must have missed these calls while rushing to blow-dry her hair. As she was about to call the professor back, an email notification popped up.

The message was very brief and from an unknown email address. It read:

"Come to Dubai right away, your old friend needs you"

There was an attachment to the email. It was a one-way ticket from DFW Airport to Dubai International Airport. The flight was this afternoon.

*****

After finishing her lecture, Jennifer returned to her hotel room in the Fairmont Dallas. She had been thinking about the email and the ticket to Dubai all day. During her lecture, she had accidently said "Dubai" instead of the name of a historical site in Greece. Her original flight back to New York was at 6:00 PM that evening. She had her bags packed and was getting ready to check out. She got a call from the bell desk that her ride to the airport had arrived. She had specifically asked the concierge to make sure that she got a sane driver this time.

At the airport, Jennifer was still unsure as to whether she should board her original flight to New York or take this other flight to Dubai. The Dubai flight was at 6:30 PM, thirty minutes after her original flight. She closed her eyes in thought for a good half of a minute. Without looking, she handed over one of the two reservations to the check-in clerk. She glanced at the boarding card that was handed to her. Then she walked toward her departure gate, heading for the destination that fate had decided for her.

Chapter 2

November 25 12:30 PM (EST)
JFK Airport, NY, USA

As Sarah was waiting to board her flight to Dubai, her thoughts went back to the mysterious message she had received a few hours back, the message that had caused her to go on a trip she would never have taken in normal circumstances.

The message was concise:

"Please come ASAP, your travel details are attached"

Being a naturally risk-averse person, Sarah normally would not have given such a message a second thought; however, in this situation, a little voice had given her courage and prompted her to make this impulsive decision. She had always trusted her little voice, and fortunately, it had never failed her.

The announcement to board her flight freaked her out for a second, but she composed herself and walked toward the plane. Upon boarding, Sarah felt suffocated and struggled for breath. Foreseeing her anxieties, she had bought some over-the-counter sleeping pills. As soon as she settled into her chair, she stopped the first air hostess that came her way.

"Excuse me, can I please have a glass of water? I am claustrophobic and need to take my medication as soon as possible."

The young air hostess, understanding the urgency in Sarah's voice, immediately brought her a glass of water and said, "Let me know if I can get you anything else."

Sarah gave her a pleasant smile and said, "Thanks, I am good for now, but please don't wake me up until the flight lands."

The air hostess took out a 'Do Not Disturb' sticker from her front pocket and placed it on Sarah's seat.

It didn't take much time for the medicine to act, and Sarah quickly fell asleep. As she was sleeping, she dreamed.

Not many people knew that Sarah was blessed with an astounding gift. She had visions of past and future events, both in her dreams and while awake. She

The Lost Miracle

preferred to keep her psychic powers a secret and only shared it with her mother and few of her close friends.

She saw herself walking in a futuristic city with an ultramodern infrastructure, unlike anything she had seen before. She saw high-speed commuter trains flying like airplanes twenty feet above the ground without physical support. As she walked along a pathway, smoke filled the air in front of her. As she emerged from the smoke, she found herself in an ancient neighborhood with houses made of clay. She entered one of the houses. Upon entering, she realized that the rooms were very small. Being claustrophobic, she ran out of the house, feeling suffocated. She ran and ran without looking back. After a few minutes, she realized that she was back in the modern city. She decided to take the train that she had seen before. She felt disoriented and accidently walked into the path of an approaching train. Sarah closed her eyes, feeling her end coming, but a hand pulled her to safety. She opened her eyes to see the face of her savior and . . .

She returned to consciousness with the announcement of their landing. The captain was requesting all passengers to return to their seats and fasten their seat belts. It felt like she had just dozed off for a few minutes, but apparently she had slept through the entire fourteen hours of her flight.

Normally, Sarah could immediately make out the hidden messages in her visions. However, this dream was very unusual and did not make sense to her — at least, not yet.

*****

November 26 5:30 PM (GST)
Dubai Airport, Dubai, UAE

A uniformed man was waiting for Sarah at Dubai Airport. When she came out of arrivals after passing through immigration and customs, she saw him holding a card with her name on it.

Sarah went up to him and said, "I'm Sarah."

The man smiled and asked her to follow him.

The Lost Miracle

After thirty minutes of driving through the beautiful Dubai skyline, Sarah reached an elaborate building that looked like a resort. She was greeted by another uniformed man who took her luggage and asked her to follow him.

As Sarah approached the long walkway that led toward reception, she was fascinated by the rich architecture of the hotel. She saw a huge aquarium with exotic sea creatures next to the stairs leading up to the reception area.

After completing the registration formalities, the receptionist handed Sarah a note that had been left for her. It said:

"Come to Dubai Marina at 9:00pm, don't be late"

The note also had an address and the name of a restaurant in Dubai Marina.

Sarah showed the note to the receptionist and asked him, "How far is this place?"

"Twenty to thirty minutes," the receptionist replied, "depending on the traffic."

Sarah looked at the clock in the reception area for the local time and realized that she had a couple of hours to freshen up.

*****

Sarah reached the restaurant on time and was escorted to her table by a pretty young Lebanese girl in traditional Arabic dress. The girl mentioned that her companion had arrived a few minutes ago. She wondered who it could be. Surely it was the person who invited her to Dubai?

Sarah almost lost her breath when she saw the person at the table. She had never expected to see her here. She asked, almost shouting, "Jen, what are you doing here?"

*****

Jennifer Riggs was as surprised as Sarah, if not more. Sarah and Jennifer had gone to the same high school and were very close friends. They looked at each other with shock and confusion. After a minute or so, Jennifer finally found her voice. She said:

"Why did you ask me to come to Dubai in such a mysterious fashion, Sarah?" Sitting back in her chair, she added, "You knew that I was coming back to New

The Lost Miracle

York and that we were supposed to meet this coming weekend."

Sarah tried to respond, but her voice was muffled by loud music and singing in Arabic, which had just commenced. The two turned in the direction of the music, and their jaws dropped wide — not from the sight of the good-looking, traditionally dressed Lebanese men doing the 'Dabke' dance, but on seeing the American man dancing with the group. He was a man that both of them knew all too well.

*****

David Solomon was the youngest son of a very rich industrialist. Dave, as he was called by his friends, had a keen interest in technology and was often seen with prototype electronic gadgets that had not yet made their way to the market. He was an outgoing person and was loved by all his friends. He carried an attractive, athletic physique. Since his teenage years, he had been an ardent fan of kickboxing and had won a few gold medals at the amateur level.

Seeing Dave in the restaurant, both Sarah and Jennifer knew who had called them to Dubai. All three of them had known each other from a young age, as

Dave had attended their high school. He had always been very unpredictable, and had played strange pranks back then.

Sarah and Jennifer couldn't wait to ask Dave why he had invited them to Dubai in such a mysterious way. They didn't wait for him to finish his dance. Fully aware of Dave's carefree nature, the girls stood up from their chairs and pulled him to the side.

Both girls were so overwhelmed that they could hardly speak. They just stared at Dave as if they would eat him alive.

Dave broke their silence. "Why are you guys staring at me like that?"

Sarah was trying to keep calm. "Don't you think you owe us an explanation?"

"Why did you invite us to Dubai like this?" Jennifer said furiously, looking Dave directly in the eyes.

Dave, trying to cool the girls down, said, "Come on, you guys have just arrived after a long flight, let's eat something, have a couple of drinks and then we can talk." He added with a smile, "The night is still young."

The girls didn't take his carefree attitude well. Jennifer made a claw-like expression using her right hand and poked her nails into Dave's abdomen. She then looked straight into his eyes and said with a firm voice:

The Lost Miracle

"We didn't come all this way to party, Mr. David Solomon." Pushing her nails deeper, she added, "You know me very well; I am going to cause some serious damage to you if you don't explain everything right now."

"Calm down, you wildcat. Save this energy. We will need it," Dave responded with a mischievous smile. Finding Jennifer very close, he kissed her gently on her forehead.

Opening his arms, Dave added, "Come on, we haven't seen each other in over five years. I need a hug before I say another word."

Surprised by this action and realizing that the three of them had not met in a very long time, the girls came close to Dave, and the three hugged briefly.

"That's a good girl." Dave suggested, "Let's go out for a walk; it's too crowded and loud inside."

*****

Chapter 3

As kids, Sarah, Jennifer, and Dave had lived in the same neighborhood in Montvale, New Jersey. They had been best friends since childhood.

After graduating from high school, Jennifer moved to New York City and went to college there. Dave went to the University of California and had been living out there ever since. The group had gotten busy with their professional lives and did not often get chances to meet up.

Dave's attitude was carefree toward everything in life. He was known for his curious nature and his special interest in mysteries. He would go to any extent to seek answers to things that fascinated him. These two traits often led him into difficult and challenging situations. Sarah and Jennifer never approved of Dave's adventures and had nicknamed him "Dave Trouble."

Once, back in their high school days, someone had told Dave that there was a fountain in Texas that cured illnesses. Dave, without adequate planning or research, had left on a road trip to find the place. On the way to Texas, he gave a ride to a beautiful female hitchhiker

The Lost Miracle

who was trying to get to California. Dave had a weakness for strangers — he often trusted them blindly. The girl took Dave to a nightclub, promising him a good time. It turned out to be a scam, and she, along with an accomplice, had robbed Dave of his money and his car.

Dave had been forced to call Sarah and Jennifer for help getting back home. It took the two a good deal of effort to find his exact location on the long route to Texas.

When they were on their way home after saving Dave from his wild adventure, Sarah had said, "Mr. Dave Trouble, we are not sure if you find troubles or troubles find you, but I am seriously worried that one day you will get all of us in serious trouble."

*****

November 26 8:30 PM (GST)
Dubai Marina, Dubai, UAE

Jennifer recalled Dave's failed trip to Texas and Sarah's comment that Dave might lead them into serious trouble one day. She wondered if this was the "serious trouble" Sarah had predicted.

Dave directed them toward a nearby bench facing the blue water, which was sparkling under the full moon, and asked them to wait for him. He then disappeared toward the parking area. Sarah and Jennifer didn't speak a word; they just kept staring at the beautiful creek.

Dave returned with a small, antique, wooden treasure chest. He placed it on the table and said, "The answer to your question is in this chest."

Their surprise increased by the ancient box in Dave's hand, the two women looked at each other. Then, Sarah moved closer to the chest, took it in her hands, and opened the lid.

It was empty.

Jennifer looked at Dave with a look that could have had many meanings, none of which would have left Dave in one piece. She tried to calm herself down, and said, "Is this your idea of a joke, Mr. Solomon?"

Dave gave them a smile and said, "Okay, let me tell you a little story." Looking at Jennifer, he added playfully, "I know some of us have a short fuse, but don't feel bad. Everyone can't be perfect like me."

Jennifer ignored Dave's comment.

The Lost Miracle

Dave started by giving them the background. "This January, shortly after New Year's eve, my father received a package from an old friend, Robert Stiavnicky."

"I take it that the package had this chest in it?" Sarah asked.

"Correct. At that time, my father thought it was a New Year's gift from his friend, and kept it in his living room." Dave carried on with a mystical tone that gave a dramatic touch to his story.

"What does all of this have to do with calling us to Dubai?" Jennifer asked.

Dave ignored her and continued. "Last month, my father came to visit me in California. He brought this for me, knowing my interest in historical artifacts."

"The only thing we have in common," Jennifer said sarcastically. Sarah gave Jennifer a look that urged her to let Dave speak.

Taking back the old wooden treasure chest from Sarah, Dave said, "You guys know that I am a big hygiene freak. I had to properly clean the thing before I placed it on the display shelf in my living room." He took a deep breath and added, "As I was cleaning it, I accidently pressed a secret button hidden on the right wall of this box. The button opens a secret chamber."

Dave pressed the same button again and showed the secret chamber to the girls. With this demonstration, he finally caught their undivided attention.

Jennifer gasped in amazement, and Sarah moved forward to peek inside. There was a triangle-shaped, ancient golden coin with a note on a small piece of leather. There was something written on the leather piece that appeared to be Arabic.

Holding the ancient leather piece and pointing toward its writing, Dave said, "This is written in Arabic. I got it translated back in California."

Dave reached the inside pocket of his jacket and handed over a piece of paper to the girls, saying, "This is the translated text."

> *"Search for a lost civilization to unleash the road to a miraculous wonder that will change the face of the earth."*

At this time, Dave picked up the triangular gold coin and pointed to the symbols of sun and sand engraved on one side and then to the other side, which was plain. He then handed over both the artifacts to Jennifer. Since she was an archeologist and a historian, Dave wanted to get her opinion.

The Lost Miracle

Jennifer took the artifacts in her hands. After inspecting them for a few minutes, she said, "One thing is for sure: the engraving on the coin does not match the age of the coin itself." She clarified, "The artifacts are probably from the Tutankhamun era, around 1332 BC–1323 BC, but the engraving on the coin and the writing on this leather piece were done recently. To me, it looks as if they were done by laser."

Jennifer, now in a relatively better mood, asked Dave, "How did you link this up with Dubai?"

"I tried speaking with Uncle Robert, the person who sent this to my dad, but he had passed away even before we received his package." Dave added, "After finding this secret chamber and these artifacts, I used all my connections across the USA and abroad to look for clues. I learned that this wooden box is one-of-a-kind, and that one of my contacts had seen it in a shop in Old Dubai."

Dave continued without even pausing to breathe. "I immediately flew to Dubai and went to that shop, but unfortunately the shop owner was not much help. They didn't even have records of who they sold the stuff to."

Dave continued in a defeated tone. "You know me very well; I can't sleep if I don't find answers to even simple mysteries. This is the most fascinating thing I have ever come across." He completed his sentence with a question. "How can I let this go?"

"I understand," said Jennifer, "but this does not explain why you brought us here in such a mysterious manner."

Dave tried to explain. "We all know that Sarah is claustrophobic. She would never have traveled such a long distance in normal circumstances." He added with a little sarcasm, "And you, Jennifer, are always on the go, giving lectures at various universities or exploring archeological sites around the world."

"Would any of you have listened to me and joined me here in Dubai?" Dave said, attempting to validate his approach.

There was a long silence, and then Sarah spoke. "It's okay. We will let you go this time." She rubbed her palms over her eyes and said, "I need to have a drink; this is too much excitement for me in one day."

The Lost Miracle

Dave looked at the fatigued faces of his two friends, realizing that they must be exhausted from the long flight. He said, "I know you guys must be tired. Let's go back to the hotel. We can discuss this further in the morning."

The girls followed Dave to the parking lot. They commenced their drive back to the hotel in Dave's rental, a black Hummer H3.

As the sturdy H3 drove through the futuristic downtown of Dubai, Sarah gazed at the towering Burj Khalifa, the tallest manmade structure in the world. She felt something strange and asked Dave to take the next exit toward the Dubai Mall. It was the world's largest shopping mall and was located right next to the Burj Khalifa.

Jennifer looked at Sarah in amazement. "What? You want to go shopping now? I thought you were tired."

Sarah didn't respond.

Dave noticed that Sarah was deeply lost in her thoughts. He knew her and her mystical powers well. Apparently, Sarah was having psychic revelations. Dave negotiated a sharp turn to take the next exit, and then turned the vehicle toward the mall entrance. As he was about to turn into the parking lot, Sarah took his hand and directed him to stop the H3 at the mall's entrance. Without saying a word, Sarah stepped out and started to walk. Dave had to stop in the no-parking zone as Sarah almost jumped out of the moving vehicle. Fortunately, he saw a valet attendant and threw the keys to him before following Sarah. Jennifer trailed behind the two without any more questions, realizing Sarah's state.

Sarah walked through the underwater zoo; she passed the mural of men diving at the waterfall inside the Dubai Mall and moved in the direction of Burj Khalifa Lake. Her thoughts kept her completely unaware of the amazing fountain show going on at that time, with water jets as high as 500 feet.

However, even in these unusual circumstances, Jennifer and Dave could not help but admire the large, incandescent fountain lights and color projectors that were creating a breathtaking visual spectrum, complimented by outstanding music.

Sarah stopped for a minute in front of the dancing fountains, closed her eyes for a few seconds, turned back and started walking again. She went back inside the mall, stopped in front of a shop, and stared at it.

Dave and Jennifer joined Sarah shortly after, and were amazed to see that the name of the shop was "Sun & Sand Sports."

Chapter 4

November 26 9:30 PM (GST)
The Dubai Mall, Dubai, UAE

The trio went inside the shop, which was empty at that time. They looked around, hoping to find something. Jennifer got frustrated and said, "It would help if we know what we are. . ." Before she could finish her sentence, she saw something, and her eyes opened wide. She could not believe what she was looking at.

Following Jennifer's gaze, Dave and Sarah looked in the same direction. On a display shelf behind the cash counter, there was an exact replica of the ancient, wooden chest with the secret compartment that Dave's father had received.

Dave approached the attractive Chinese girl at the counter. She had long, straight black hair and an innocent face with a cute little nose. Dave said, "Hi, what is the price of that chest on the shelf behind you?" He pointed toward the artifact.

The Chinese girl replied in perfect, unaccented English, "Sorry, this is not for sale. I can certainly help you with something else."

Sarah came forward and asked the girl, "Hi, can I ask for your name?"

"Fen," the Chinese girl replied.

Sarah asked, "Fen, is there another Chinese lady who works here?" Sarah closed her eyes as if in a deep trance and continued to describe the other lady. "I am referring to another Chinese women more or less the same height as you are, but twenty-five to thirty years older than you. I don't know her Chinese name, but I think the meaning of her name in English is Orchid."

Fen's expression changed upon hearing Sarah's description. She asked with a skeptical tone, "You have just described my mother, Ching Lan." Fen paused for a few seconds and added, "How do you know her? Who are you guys?"

"Don't be afraid of us, Fen. We are friends," Dave explained, trying to calm the girl down. "We came from the USA, and we need to meet her. Can we please speak with her?"

Dave noticed that Fen's eyes were wet with tears.

Fen responded, "My mother passed away last month."

The Lost Miracle

*****

Sarah came closer to Fen, held her hands to comfort her, and said, "We are really sorry to hear of your loss." She tried to look into Fen's eyes, but Fen kept looking down, trying to control her emotions.

It took Fen a full minute to get ahold of herself. She wiped her tears using a tissue provided by Sarah and said, "My father is in the back office. Would you like to talk to him?"

Dave didn't take a second to respond. He said, "It would be great if we could meet him."

Fen called her father using the intercom and spoke to him in Mandarin. She looked up at the trio and said, "My father needs to complete some work; he says he can see you in thirty minutes." Fen added, "You can wait here in the shop if you like."

Jennifer responded, "Thanks. We will wait in that coffee shop opposite your store."

After they settled down in the coffee shop, Sarah asked, "Dave, where is our wooden chest? We may need to show it to Fen's father."

Dave pointed to a small bag he was carrying.

Before they could finish their coffee, Fen walked into the cafe and announced that her father was ready to see them. They immediately stood up and followed Fen. Her father was waiting for them at the counter. Sarah and Jennifer noticed that the second wooden chest was missing from where they had seen it last.

Fen introduced her father to them, saying that his name was Alan Chow. Dave extended his hand to Alan, but Alan turned around without speaking a word and started walking. Fen asked them to follow her father.

Following Fen's father, Dave wondered how to begin the conversation and what it would take to convince him to sell the artifact.

Alan was a thin, tall man; even with all-white hair, he didn't look that old. He was wearing round glasses with silver metal frames. Upon entering his office, Alan sat down in his black revolving chair and, with a gesture, asked the trio to take a seat.

Alan took off his glasses and placed them on his small mahogany desk, then spoke with an accent. "What can I do for you?"

"We would like to buy the old wooden chest that was behind your main counter," Dave replied, getting straight to business.

"I believe my daughter made it clear that it is not for sale." Alan was firm in his tone.

"But. . ." Jennifer tried to speak, but Alan cut her off.

"It belongs to someone else," he said.

Dave wanted to ask who, but Sarah squeezed his arm to keep him quiet. He wondered if she was reading his mind.

The Lost Miracle

Alan looked at Sarah and asked her, "How do you know my wife?"

"I don't," Sarah responded.

"Then how could you describe her so well?"

Sarah had always found it difficult to explain her mystical gift. She preferred to keep her clairvoyance a secret. She didn't know how to respond.

Jennifer's and Dave's experience with Sarah's gift was the reason that they had followed her into the Dubai Mall without asking any questions. They were aware that Sarah did not like telling people about her gift.

Jennifer sensed Sarah's discomfort and made an effort to change the topic. Taking the wooden chest out of Dave's bag, she said, "We would like to show you something."

She placed the chest in front of Alan on his mahogany table.

Alan's eyes opened wide with shock. For a second, he thought that the trio had stolen his chest. He pushed his chair back and rolled it toward a side table on his right. Bending down, he opened the drawer and was visibly surprised to see his wooden chest still there. He turned to the visitors and tried to speak, but was interrupted by Jennifer. She started to tell the story of Dave's father receiving the first wooden chest, but she in turn was cut short by Sarah, who squeezed her hand, warning her not to reveal any critical details.

"My wife told me that you would be coming, but I was expecting someone else," Alan mumbled, looking at Dave. Apparently, he hadn't paid any attention to what Jennifer was saying. He added, "Someone older than you."

Dave realized that Alan must be referring to his father's friend Rob, who had sent the first wooden chest to his father. He said, "You are probably referring to my Uncle Rob."

Unable to judge Alan's expression, Dave spoke his next sentence cautiously. "He is the one who sent us on this expedition."

Lost in his thoughts, Alan took a whole minute before responding. "Last year, Robert came to our shop and left this chest with my wife. He went to the same university in the USA as my wife, and they were close friends." Alan picked up his glasses from the mahogany table, put them back on, and added: "Robert asked my wife to protect this chest and to give it to his friend, who would bring with him a key."

Upon completing his sentence, Alan began a detailed inspection of the chest that Dave had brought in.

"What key?" Jennifer asked quizzically.

Sarah thought for a second, then took out the golden triangle coin from her pocket and handed it to Alan. She had kept it close to herself, hoping to connect with its aura and learn more about it using her mystical powers.

Looking at the triangular artifact, Alan's eyes lit up and a smile replaced the frown on his face.

"This is it," Alan said. "Robert told me that there would be an ancient, triangular piece of gold with symbols of sun and sand engraved on its face."

Alan then bent to the side table, where the second wooden chest was kept, and took the chest out. Placing the second chest on the desk, he said, "It is all yours."

*****

The trio couldn't believe their luck. They had not been expecting to make progress so quickly and had not known how they might find this second clue. Fortunately, the sequence of events had turned in their favor. They couldn't wait to open the second chest and find out the next clue. They nearly ran back to the entrance where they had left their Hummer. The valet brought it back for them from the lower ground level of the cinema car park.

Once they were back in the vehicle, Jennifer opened the chest. It was empty, but they were relieved to see a similar latch for a secret compartment. This wooden chest had another triangular gold coin that more or less looked to be from the same era. However, the engraving on its face was different.

This second coin had an inscription of fire engraved on it.

The triangular gold coin was accompanied by another note. This time, the note was on a piece of cloth with some traditional designs on its border.

Jennifer read the note aloud:

The Lost Miracle

> *"The lost civilization is closer than you think."*

After inspecting this new set of clues, Jennifer said, "There are a quite a few civilizations that have mysteriously disappeared from the face of earth, but the closest to us in terms of distance is the Indus Valley Civilization." She added, with bit of worry in her voice, "The problem is, it's in Pakistan."

*****

Chapter 5

Dave almost drove the SUV into the curb upon hearing the word Pakistan. He said, "These days, that is one of the most dangerous places on Earth to visit."

Sarah inspected the artwork on the cloth accompanying the second gold coin, and said, "You are right, Jen. I have studied the art of the subcontinent, and this does look like it was made in Pakistan."

Sarah recalled her dream in the plane, in which she had seen herself walking in an ultramodern, futuristic city and then passed through smoke to find herself in an ancient town. She realized that this was an indication of her coming to the ultramodern Dubai and then going to find the lost civilization of the Indus Valley.

Still shaking his head at this recent piece of information, Dave said, "It is too dangerous to go there. I can't risk your lives."

He took another minute to think and then said, "I'll arrange for your return flights back to the states. I will have to make the rest of the trip alone."

"No, I will go with you," Sarah said. With her eyes closed, she continued, "I had a vision while on my flight to Dubai. I know this is something very important, and I have to come along."

After a few seconds, Sarah added, "I am sure you will need my help. The clues alone are not clear enough." She was firm in her statement.

Jennifer looked at Sarah with her eyes wide. She knew Sarah too well and was aware that Sarah preferred to stay miles away from trouble.

Looking at Jennifer's surprised face, Sarah narrated the dream that she had during her flight to meet Dave and Jennifer. After listening to Sarah's dream and her commitment to go on even in the face of known and present danger, Jennifer said:

"If Sarah is not afraid to go there, count me in." She added, "I am an archeologist and have had a desire to see the Indus Civilization ruins myself but never got a chance."

Dave knew that he would not be able to make any progress without Sarah and Jennifer. He didn't resist further. He said, "Okay, but we will have to take precautions."

"What do you have in mind?" asked Jennifer.

Dave gave her a mischievous smile and said, "Have patience sweetheart, you will find out in the morning."

Changing the topic, Sarah asked Jennifer, "What is the Indus Valley Civilization?"

Jennifer responded, "According to historical records, the Indus Valley Civilization was a Bronze Age civilization spread across what today is northeast Afghanistan to Pakistan and northwest India. It flourished in the basins of the Indus River, one of the major rivers of Asia, and the Ghaggar-Hakra River, which once coursed through northwest India and eastern Pakistan."

Dave said, "Sounds like it must be big."

Jennifer replied, "True; at its peak, the Indus Civilization is estimated to have had a population of over five million."

"What did they do for a living?" Sarah inquired.

Jennifer, showing off her knowledge of history, said, "The inhabitants of the ancient Indus River Valley developed new techniques in handicrafts and metallurgy and earned their livelihood utilizing these skills."

Jennifer added, "It is interesting that the Indus cities had advanced urban planning for their time, with baked brick houses, elaborate drainage systems, water supply systems, and clusters of large non-residential buildings."

The Lost Miracle

Dave looked at Jennifer. Apparently not too excited with all this historic background, he tried to change the topic. "I know you can talk about history all night, but I am starving and need to eat something fast."

"I wouldn't stop you this time Dave, I am also starving," Sarah replied.

"I'm in," Jennifer said. Looking at Dave, she asked, "Do you know any good restaurants that would be open at this hour?"

Dave smiled and said, "This is Dubai; everything is open at this hour." He checked the rearview mirror and changed lanes to take the exit toward Jumeirah Beach.

"I know just the place to take you guys," he said with confidence.

In Jumeirah, Dave stopped the car in front of an upscale beachfront restaurant and bar. The place was crowded with people of various nationalities. Dubai being a multicultural city, people of many cultures and ethnicities could be found more or less everywhere you went. The trio ordered a three-course meal and enjoyed hip music in English, Spanish, and Arabic.

Throughout the dinner, they spoke only when ordering food and asking for the check. After reaching their hotel, they went straight to their rooms to retire for the night.

Tony Agha

*****

November 27 8:30 AM (GST)
Dubai, UAE

The trio agreed to meet at 8:00 AM at their hotel's breakfast buffet. Jennifer was the first to arrive at the signature restaurant; she was always an early riser. She was very impressed to see the elaborate buffet table. It was probably one of the grandest breakfast buffets she had ever seen. Being a health freak, she normally ate only healthy stuff; however, today was an exception.

Sarah joined Jennifer when she was inspecting the mouthwatering dishes at the buffet. Sarah asked, "Dave is late again?"

Before Jennifer could reply, they heard Dave's voice. "How can both of you look so beautiful even this early in the morning?" Dave was casually dressed in white t-shirt and light blue jeans.

Sarah and Jennifer were poles apart when it came to dress and makeup. Sarah was her simple self, wearing a simple yet sexy top with an allover rose print and scoop back along with white jeans.

Jennifer stood out in a graphic, monochrome white dress from Lauren Santo Domingo's Valentino. Ravishing beauty was a common attribute in both of them; no matter what they wore, they looked stunning.

"I have everything sorted out," Dave announced, filling his plate from the buffet table.

"Fortunately, I have a very close friend in the Pakistani consulate who has kindly expedited our visa processing. We should get our visas at the Dubai Airport before we board our flight to Karachi this afternoon." Dave spoke with a touch of pride in his voice and added, looking at his wristwatch, "As soon as we finish our breakfast, we have to go and do some shopping."

"What kind of shopping?" Jennifer asked.

"First of all, we will have to dress up as locals to avoid standing out as foreigners." Dave explained, "I have located a couple of Pakistani clothes outlets in Deira, Dubai; we should be able to get something for all of us there."

Tony Agha

*****

It was taking Jennifer longer than expected to buy clothes. Dave commented, "Why are you taking so long? We are not going for a fashion show, and you hardly know anything about Pakistani fashion, so just buy anything."

Jennifer ignored Dave and selected her dresses carefully.

After buying clothes from the Pakistani boutique, Dave took them to the nearby Deira City Center Mall — they didn't have enough time to visit any of the newer malls.

Dave stopped in front of a makeup shop and said, "We need to buy darker shade concealers that will make our skin tones look wheatish."

"Jennifer, you will have to color your hair dark brown." Dave directed her to a nearby hair salon.

Jennifer didn't complain. She knew that she would stand out as a blonde in Pakistan.

The Lost Miracle

After shopping, they had no time to spare before the flight. The trio quickly packed their stuff and reached Dubai Airport just in time to pick up their visas and board the flight to Karachi.

While waiting in the boarding lounge, Dave informed the two, "Fortunately, my father does business with a very influential Pakistani businessman who was kind enough to arrange transportation and an armed guard for our protection."

As Dave completed his sentence, the flight crew announced commencement of boarding for their flight.

Little did Dave know that things don't always turn out the way we plan them.

Chapter 6

November 27 6:00 PM (PST)
Quaid-e-Azam International Airport, Karachi

Their flight was pleasant, and Dave was especially happy with the cute air hostess. He was very close to getting her number after landing, but she was called into the cabin by the captain. Dave cursed the captain, and the trio moved on. After passing through immigration at the Karachi airport, the trio put on their Pakistani clothes and applied the concealer to darken their skin tones for a wheatish look. Dave had suggested that they go through immigration in their normal attire to avoid any cross-questioning by the immigration authorities.

The weather was refreshing, around 74°F, with a clear sky. Jennifer noticed a well-dressed man wearing a black suit with a white shirt and a light blue tie, holding a card with Dave's name. She directed the group toward him.

"Hi, I'm Dave." Dave put his hand forward for a handshake.

The gentleman looked a bit surprised at their appearance, with their dark skin tones and local clothing, and said, "I was expecting Americans." He thought for a second, and then said, "Oh, I get it, you must have migrated to the USA, or your parents must be from South Asia." Dave didn't feel like giving any explanations and stayed quiet.

"Anyway, welcome to Karachi, my name is Atif Khan." Atif waved to a porter standing nearby to take their luggage, which was only hand carry.

Atif appeared to be in his early 30s. He acted in a very formal manner, like he was from a professional services firm, and definitely unlike the conventional armed guard that the trio had been expecting.

"You guys travel light," Atif commented, looking at their luggage.

"We are here for a short trip," Dave responded.

A valet parked a white Toyota Land Cruiser in front of them.

As they were being seated, Jennifer could not control herself. She said to Atif, "You don't look like an armed guard."

Surprised by her comment, Atif waited for the porter to finish loading the luggage in the Land Cruiser before responding. "I apologize, I should have introduced myself first." Atif spoke while searching for the ticket that he needed to exit the airport parking. "I work for Mr. Rehman Zaman, who owns a number of industries in Pakistan; I am the marketing manager for one of his companies." After pausing for a few seconds, Atif continued, "I believe Dave's family knows him."

Jennifer, concerned about the group's security, said with a sarcastic tone, "If I am not mistaken, we were supposed to be provided with armed guards here in Pakistan."

Atif ignored the sarcasm in Jennifer's tone. "Don't worry, we have arranged two ex-army officials to accompany you for your trip. Mr. Zaman didn't want to take any chances, so he asked his trusted security company in Islamabad to provide guards for you." Atif continued, with confidence and pride in his voice, "They specialize in protecting VIPs."

"I don't see anyone here," Jennifer said, again sarcastically.

"Unfortunately, their flight from Islamabad got delayed," Atif responded defensively.

"Mr. Zaman is out of country with his family. He asked me to pick you up from the airport and drop you at the Marriott Hotel." Recognizing the group's concern about their security in Karachi, Atif added, "Don't worry, the guards will be with you shortly after we reach the hotel. The Marriott Hotel is located in a very safe place right next to the US Consulate."

The Lost Miracle

Before Jennifer could complain any further, Atif's phone rang. He took the call using his Bluetooth earpiece. The call didn't last long, and Atif hung up with an expression of utter concern. He started to perspire even with the cool air blowing out of the air conditioner.

Jennifer felt bad for being too harsh on the poor guy; it was not his fault. He was just an employee, brought into this situation by his boss and by circumstances beyond his control.

She pulled out a tissue from a box lying close to her and said, "I am sorry. I didn't mean to make you uncomfortable."

Jennifer handed the tissue to Atif and added, "Here, please wipe your face with this. There is no need to be worried, we will not complain to your boss."

"It's not that." Atif paused for a couple of seconds. Wiping the sweat from his forehead, he said, "Something really terrible has happened."

"What happened?" Dave asked.

Atif didn't know how to explain the situation to someone who was coming to Karachi for the very first time. The visitors probably had no knowledge of what the city could go through in situations that were not half as bad as what had just happened.

Atif started giving them background about the current situation in Pakistan. "I am not sure if you are aware that we are about to have general elections in Pakistan. A leader of one of the strongest political parties, who happened to be an ex-prime minister of Pakistan, recently returned to the country from a very long, self-imposed exile."

Dave nodded his head. "Yes, I know. She was living in London and Dubai. I follow world news very religiously." He added, "Especially news about powerful political characters like her. She is a very graceful lady, and I believe she is an Oxford University graduate."

"Then you may know that she is deeply loved by a large faction of the people, especially in this province of Sindh." Atif hoped to convey the gravity of the situation.

Dave nodded.

"She has just been killed, shot by an unidentified person in Rawalpindi as she was coming back from a political rally." Atif added, with a lot of fear in his voice, "and now the whole country, especially Karachi, is under a significant security threat. Unknown people are burning vehicles and shops."

"We can't go to the hotel, all the roads are blocked. We will have to turn away from the city and seek refuge until things get sane."

*****

The Lost Miracle

As Atif was looking at his options for a safe route, Sarah brought the group's attention to a mob of people running toward their SUV with iron bars and fire torches in their hands.

Atif slammed on the brakes of the Land Cruiser. When the speed dropped to about twenty-five miles per hour, he pulled the hand break and turned the wheel. The SUV turned 180 degrees to face the wrong side of the road. Atif negotiated the oncoming cars, who were also trying to change their routes and save themselves from the mob.

Atif drove over the curb to the other side of the road. Now back on the correct side, he drove with the traffic.

Straight ahead, they saw another mob burning a passenger bus. Atif turned the Land Cruiser into a narrow side street and away from the main road.

After driving for a few minutes and taking numerous turns, Atif was perspiring even more than before. It seemed that they were still not in a safe zone.

"Can we just go to a police station?" Jennifer asked Atif.

Shaking his head, Atif said, "I am not from this part of the city and don't know if there is one close by."

"Do you know where you are going?" Dave asked.

"No," Atif replied, keeping his eyes on the road.

Recognizing that they didn't have a lot of options, the visiting trio chose not to be vocal about their concerns.

After a few more minutes of driving, Sarah saw that they were surrounded by cattle farms, mostly buffalo, on both sides of the road. She asked Atif, "What is this place?"

Atif replied, "This is called Landhi Dairy Colony, commonly known in the local language as Bhains Colony."

"This place is huge," Sarah commented.

"It is the world's largest buffalo colony, spread over 1,600 acres with around 400,000 animals." Atif sounding more like a tour guide than a marketing manager. He added, "Let's take refuge here. We can hide our car behind the buffalo."

Atif drove the Land Cruiser slowly and parked it behind a herd of buffalo so that they were not visible from the road. He then called someone to get an update on the situation.

After finishing his call, he said, "Some more bad news for you, guys — the situation is getting worse. We can't go back to the city until things calm down. The plane that was bringing in your armed guards didn't take off from Islamabad. The capitol is on alert because of this incident in Rawalpindi, an adjoining city."

"Oh no!" Dave exclaimed with shock.

The Lost Miracle

Atif, trying to hide his own fear, said, "Don't worry, Mr. Zaman's secretary is arranging for local armed guards from another company in Karachi."

"We know you are trying your best under the circumstances," Dave quickly said. He had feared that Jennifer might blurt out some sarcastic comment, which might tick off this poor guy, who was as much a victim of the situation as they were.

Jennifer, on the contrary, said politely, "Don't worry, it's okay. We didn't get a chance to introduce ourselves at the airport — my name is Jennifer." She offered Atif a handshake. Then, pointing to Dave and Sarah, she added, "This cute, innocent girl is Sarah, and this crazy guy is Dave."

Dave and Sarah gave each other a surprised look. Jennifer's sudden change of mood was unexpected, especially under these circumstances.

"What do you think, Atif? How long will it take for things to settle down?" Dave asked.

Atif responded, shaking his head, "No idea." After thinking for a few seconds, he added, "To be very honest with you, it looks like we will have to spend the night in the car. Alternatively, we can try and find a hotel outside the city."

Dave thought for a minute. He realized that it might not be worth wasting time here in Karachi. Using the softest voice he could find within, he asked Atif, "I apologize pulling you into this, but we don't have a lot of time and we need to get to the region of the Indus Valley Civilization. Can you please take us there?" He added, "It will probably be safer there."

"The Indus Valley Civilization was spread across northeast Afghanistan to Pakistan and northwest India. Where exactly do you want to go?" Atif asked Dave.

Before Dave could say anything, Jennifer replied, "Mohenjo-daro."

Dave and Sarah were surprised with Jennifer's reply. The trio had not discussed this before, and their last clue had only narrowed their search to the entire Indus Valley Civilization.

Reading their minds, Jennifer clarified. "I did some research using my laptop in the plane. I figured out that the designs on the border of the piece of cloth that we found in Dubai resemble a lot of the artifacts discovered in Mohenjo-daro."

"What is Mohenjo-daro?" Dave asked.

Jennifer explained, "Mohenjo-daro means 'Mound of the Dead' in English. It is an archeological site in the province of Sindh, Pakistan that was built around 2600 BCE."

Trying to assess whether Dave was following her explanation, she continued, "It was one of the largest settlements of the ancient Indus Valley Civilization and one of the world's earliest major urban settlements. Interestingly, Mohenjo-daro was abandoned in the 19th century BCE and was not rediscovered until 1922."

"What piece of cloth and designs?" Atif asked with a puzzled tone, ignoring the historical background of Mohenjo-daro. "I don't think I completely understand what you guys are talking about."

Dave, realizing that they needed Atif for any chance of reaching Mohenjo-daro, related the whole story to him. Atif listened with great excitement. As Dave was about to finish, they were startled by a loud knock on Atif's window.

There was an elderly man wearing a long, white shirt with a long piece of cloth around his waist. These were called dhoti kurta in the local language and were a traditional men's garment for milk vendors in Pakistan.

The guy said something in a regional language and stepped back. Atif turned back to face the group.

Atif told them, "He is saying that this is private property and we can't stay here, so we will have to leave."

Chapter 7

November 27 7:00 PM (PST)
Landhi Dairy Colony, a.k.a. Bhains Colony, Karachi

As Atif started the SUV and pushed the manual transmission into first gear, he said to the group, "Mohenjo-daro is around five hours drive from here."

Once on the road, he warned the trio, "You should know that the route to Mohenjo-daro is not safe, as we have to pass through the town of Noori-abad and Dadu District." He went on, "These areas are considered to be notorious dacoit havens."

Sarah asked, "What is a Dacoit?"

Atif clarified. "Dacoit is a local term used for a group of people who carry out organized robberies and murder."

Dave smiled and joked, "Considering the prevailing conditions, we might be safer in the dacoit haven than in Karachi."

The Lost Miracle

Atif knew that Dave's lighthearted comment was probably true; they had nowhere to take refuge near the city and might well be better off staying away from Karachi.

He contemplated possible scenarios in his head and decided to go for the unknown danger. He turned the vehicle toward Mohenjo-daro.

Prior to embarking on the long journey, Atif stopped on the curb side to check the route with his phone.

He selected the best possible route and announced, "I have good news and bad news." He took a second to make sure that he had everyone's undivided attention and continued. "The good news is that I can take a detour away from Noori-abad to avoid the first danger zone. The bad news is we may still have to pass through Dadu, which is a major hub of robberies and murder."

No one said anything in response as there had been few options in the first place.

After driving for a couple of hours, Atif said to the group, "If you guys are hungry, I can stop at the next dhaba." Realizing that no one would have understood what a dhaba was, he explained, "Dhaba is the generic name for a roadside restaurant."

All three responded at the same time. "No, let's just keep going."

They kept driving for the next three hours or so. Atif had to stop once for gas. Sarah fell asleep in the back seat. Meanwhile, Jennifer and Dave kept talking with Atif to keep him awake. They were afraid that he might fall asleep on this dark and secluded highway.

After dozing off, Sarah had another dream.

She saw herself in a small village house with Dave and Jennifer at her side. The house had a style of construction that she had never seen before. The walls were light brown and made of clay with a wood-framed roof that had been covered using large palm leaves. Outside, the front wall had some round, black stuff pasted on it. There was a very old tree in front of the house. She was talking to a middle-aged man, who spoke a language that she had heard before but could not understand.

There was another man standing close to her, interpreting the discussion between Sarah and this middle-aged man. She could not see his face.

Another vision overcame this one. Now, she was in a somewhat bigger house built with concrete. She was in a large room with her friends, and a very bright light appeared in the center of that room . . .

The Lost Miracle

*She heard someone calling her name . . .
Sarah . . . Sarah . . .*

Sarah opened her eyes and saw Dave addressing her.

"Sarah, were you asleep? I am so sorry, I didn't realize that you were sleeping." Dave offered her a can of Coke and a pack of potato chips that Atif had just bought from a gas station.

Sarah had not been in a deep sleep, but she was upset at not being able to see the complete vision. She responded negatively to the Coke and potato chips, shaking her head and replying with a gentle smile, "It's okay, I'm good."

Sarah looked around and noticed that they were driving on a two-lane highway, with one lane moving each way and no partition in the center. Dave was eating his potato chips like a young boy during a school lunch break. Atif and Jennifer were having a conversation. She heard Atif say:

"These highways are very dangerous, especially during the night. If anyone has to travel after sunset, they request police to accompany them through this stretch of the road." Atif added, "Since our trip was not pre-planned and with the current law and order situation in the big cities, we couldn't get police protection."

"I hope we stay safe," Jennifer commented.

Atif continued with his story. "For common people, that protection is not easily available. If a passenger bus is robbed, they block the entire highway until the police arrive. If they don't block the traffic, the police may not show up for a long time."

Sara's eyes caught something lying on the middle of the road ahead. It was a donkey cart, overloaded with square bales of hay. The cart was blocking the highway around 300 meters from their current position, and there were two men trying to push it. She heard Dave speak.

"Hey, look ahead, it looks like their cart is stuck." He added, "Do they need help?"

"Could this be a trap?" Jennifer commented, not agreeing with Dave and somewhat scared from all the stories that Atif had told.

"I agree with Jennifer," said Atif. "I have heard so many horror stories of this area. Let's just keep going." He slowed the Land Cruiser but didn't stop. He took the vehicle onto the unpaved shoulder and bypassed the donkey cart.

Shortly after they had passed the cart, they heard some gunshots fired in their direction. Atif looked in his rearview mirror and shouted, flooring the gas pedal at the same time.

"Stay low, everyone," he warned, sounding very scared. "It was a trap. They are firing at us."

The Lost Miracle

The huge SUV did not respond to the gas pedal as quickly as they were hoping. On the bright side, however, the distance between them and the shooters was increasing with every passing second.

Dave had always been interested in firearms and was familiar with most firearms used around the globe. He had been able to peek at the shooter's weapon at the beginning of the ordeal and informed everyone of his expert opinion. "I think we are out of range. They are firing with very old rifles. I am positive that they can't cause any damage from this distance."

The group sighed with relief as they listened to this information. However, their sense of security wouldn't last for long. Jennifer brought their attention to a couple of motorcycles parked ahead of them. They had not noticed them until they were very close because the riders had turned their lights off.

*****

As the Land Cruiser came closer to the waiting motorcycles, the drivers turned their lights on and moved in the direction of the approaching SUV.

Atif knew that his heavy vehicle would not be able to match the quick pick-up speed of the street bikes. He turned sharply, taking the SUV off the road. They tore through a thick stand of wild plants. Dave, Jennifer, and Sarah grabbed the side handles to keep themselves in their seats as the Land Cruiser jumped up and down on the rough terrain.

The only thing in their favor was the Land Cruiser's ability to tackle extreme off-road conditions. The vehicle drove through thick bushes and over uneven ground with ease. Fortunately, after a couple of minutes, Atif was able to find an unpaved road — really more like a dirt track.

Sarah looked back. She saw faint lights coming from the attackers' motorcycles, and said, "We are gaining distance on them."

Atif pointed Jennifer to a compass fixed on the dashboard of his vehicle. She was now the officially designated co-driver of this nighttime desert safari.

"Jennifer," Atif said, "please keep an eye on the compass and make sure that we are going north." Atif added, "I have to concentrate on this dirt track."

"Yes, sure," Jennifer responded, straightening up in her seat. "I can do that."

After about ten minutes, Sarah looked back and noticed that the motorcycles' lights were not visible anymore. She said excitedly, "It looks like we have lost the attackers!" She gave Dave a high five.

The Lost Miracle

Atif and Jennifer were concentrating on driving in the right direction without getting into more trouble. Atif had mentioned that these dirt tracks often branched out and that the two branches might lead to totally different locations miles apart from each other.

After driving for around two and a half hours, they saw lights, apparently coming from a nearby town or a village. Atif kept driving in the direction of the lights.

It took them another thirty minutes to find a paved road leading to that nearby town.

Upon reaching the town, they saw a roadside restaurant. There were around ten bedsteads of woven webbing stretched on four-legged wooden frames. These were placed in groups of two with tables in between. They saw a small group of people eating and another group watching television.

Stopping the car in front of the restaurant, Atif said, "I'll go and ask these people where we are and how to get to Mohenjo-daro."

The trio watched Atif as he chatted with a couple of locals. They were making hand gestures, probably to confirm directions. It took him fifteen minutes to return. Instead of coming inside, he walked around the Land Cruiser, apparently inspecting the tires.

"There may be a slow puncture in our rear left tire," he said, opening the front door on Jennifer's side. "The guy I was talking to pointed it out; he is a mechanic and he can fix it in thirty minutes."

Placing his right hand on his stomach, Atif added, "I don't know about you guys, but I am starving. I would like to grab a bite."

"Me, too," Jennifer said, looking back at Dave and Sarah. "I need to eat something real fast, otherwise I'll faint."

Dave and Sarah nodded in agreement, and they got out of the vehicle.

The group settled down at a table away from the rest of the crowd.

"Is he going to bring the menu?" Dave asked Atif.

Atif replied with a smile, "They don't have printed menus at roadside restaurants." He added, "I spoke to the waiter and he told me tonight's specials: chicken and goat karahi, cooked in a wok with strong spices, tomatoes, and capsicum; chicken pilaf, which is rice boiled with chicken stock and pieces of chicken with light seasoning; mixed vegetables; and last but not least, lentils."

It didn't take long for their food to arrive.

Dave asked, "Atif, do you know what this place is called and how far we are from our destination?"

"This place is called Naushahro Firoze, and we are still around two hours away from Mohenjo-daro," Atif replied.

Dave noticed that Sarah was not listening to their conversation. Instead, she was staring at a man sitting about ten feet away from them.

The Lost Miracle

Dave couldn't help but ask Sarah, "Is everything okay? You seem a bit lost."

Sarah described the vision that she had seen a few hours back in the car. When she finished, she said, "You see that man sitting over there? He looks exactly like the middle-aged man from my dream."

*****

Chapter 8

November 28 12:30 AM (PST)
Naushahro Firoze, Sindh, Pakistan

The middle-aged man was warming himself alone near a campfire. He was smoking a "hookah," a water pipe with tobacco and a burning coal fire on top. It was similar to the famous Arabic "shisha," which used flavored tobacco.

"We should go and talk to him," Dave said.

"Yeah, I agree. But we have to be careful not to scare him off or create a scene," Jennifer warned.

"I agree with Jennifer. I'll go and ask him some general question, as a traveler," Atif said.

Atif took another bite of the chicken from his plate and stood up to go and speak with the guy.

Sarah and rest of the team observed him from where they were seated.

Upon returning, Atif said, "His name is Shakir. He is a firewood vendor specializing in delivering firewood to remote locations in Northern Sindh."

Recalling the inscriptions on the second gold coin, Dave said, "Oh my God, are you guys thinking what I am thinking?" He added, "Remember, on the second gold coin, there was an inscription of fire."

While Jennifer's eyes lit up with excitement, Sarah's didn't show as much enthusiasm. She had already known from her vision that there was a link between Shakir and the second clue.

Jennifer asked Atif, "Were you able to find a link between Shakir and Mohenjo-daro?"

"Shakir delivers firewood to travelers visiting Mohenjo-daro," Atif replied.

Sarah finally spoke. "Can we talk to him?"

"Shakir mentioned that he has had a very rough day and is trying to gather his strength to go back home," Atif responded.

"Then maybe we can offer him a lift?" Dave suggested.

"Good idea!" Jennifer exclaimed.

Atif thought for a minute and said, "Okay, I'll ask him for directions to a hotel or rest house and then offer to drop him at his home."

They waited for the mechanic to fix the tire. Atif went back to Shakir and said something in Urdu, the national language of Pakistan. Atif mentioned that

Shakir's mother tongue was Sindhi but that he could understand and speak Urdu. Atif didn't speak Sindhi, and it would have been tough to communicate otherwise.

Sarah felt a sigh of relief when she saw Shakir following Atif to their SUV.

Shakir entered the vehicle from the rear door and found himself a place to sit by adjusting the luggage.

"Atif, can you inquire with him whether an American visited Mohenjo-daro in the last year and left some artifact?" Sarah requested.

Atif nodded and translated Sarah's question for Shakir as he steered the vehicle back toward the main road.

Shakir replied in Urdu, which only Atif could understand.

"The guy has a sarcastic sense of humor," Atif said, and then he translated Shakir's response. "He is mocking the question and saying that many visitors from around the world have visited these ruins. He doesn't go around and ask them for their passports before giving them firewood."

Jennifer said with sarcasm in her tone, "Can you ask this funny guy if anyone, regardless of their nationality, left something that is to be given to a specific individual?"

Atif asked Shakir and shook his head after hearing his response. He said, "Shakir is saying no one left anything."

Sarah showed one of the wooden chests and the two gold coins to Shakir and asked him directly, "Do these mean anything to you?"

Shakir looked in Atif's direction, listened to the translation, and shook his head.

Dave asked Sarah, "Are you sure he is the guy?" He added, "I don't think this guy knows anything."

Then Shakir asked Atif to stop the vehicle, as they were in front of his house. Shakir got out of the vehicle and walked toward the house.

Sarah recognized the house. It looked exactly like the first house from her vision. She was not giving up. She got out of the vehicle and said loudly, "Shakir Shah, you are a Syed, which is a very respectable thing. I know Syeds don't lie . . . for the love of your daughter, Mahnoor, please help us." She added, "I know you have something for us that you have been holding for about a year now."

Shakir's eyes opened wide. He did not speak English but could understand four words: Shakir Shah, Syed, and Mahnoor.

How could this stranger, who didn't even speak his language, know his full name, his honorary title, and his daughter's name?

Shakir stopped, turned back, and looked into Sarah's eyes for a good thirty seconds. Then he looked at Atif, apparently expecting a translation.

Atif was even more surprised than Shakir, and before he translated for Shakir, he asked Sarah, "How do you know his full name, his daughter's name, and that he is a Syed? He never told this to any of us."

Sarah never liked bragging about or giving explanations of her psychic powers. Ignoring Atif's question, she said, "Please, just translate what I said for Shakir."

Reluctantly, Atif obliged.

Shakir asked him the same question. "How does she know?"

Sarah knew what was coming and before Atif could translate Shakir's question, she said, "Atif, please tell him the complete story with all the details." After pausing for a couple of seconds, she added, "We need his help."

Dave had exited the SUV by this time. He held Atif's arm with a gesture to wait and asked Sarah, "Are you sure we can trust him?" Concerned, he added, "We hardly know this guy."

Sarah nodded and said, looking into Dave's eyes, "Trust me. I know what I am doing."

Dave released his grip on Atif's arm and gave him a nod. Atif walked closer to Shakir and asked him if they could sit somewhere. Shakir took them inside their house. His daughter was at the door now having heard her father. Shakir introduced the group to his daughter and asked her to bring some refreshments for the guests.

The inside of the house was exactly like the one Sarah had seen in her dream.

Atif narrated the whole story to Shakir. After listening to everything quietly, Shakir stood up and started to walk without saying a word. He went outside the house and into his backyard. Surprised, the group followed him.

Shakir stopped near an old tree and started digging with his bare hands. After digging for fifteen minutes, his hands struck something. Shakir pulled out a rectangular metal box. He cleared the dirt from the box and brought it back inside the house. The box was closed with a bolt and secured with a heavy iron lock.

Shakir placed the box in the center of the room and said something in Urdu, which Atif translated.

"Shakir says that a middle-aged Caucasian man with long, gray hair, blue eyes, and a thin body visited Mohenjo-daro last year." He continued, "He knew the guy, as he had previously visited Mohenjo-daro with an international tour group a couple of years back."

Atif paused for a minute to take the teacup from Shakir's daughter, who had just entered the room. She carried the tea in small, white cups without handles.

With them, she brought some delicious, homemade cumin cookies.

Pointing toward Shakir's daughter, Atif said, "Mahnoor is Shakir's only daughter and a graduate from Punjab University." Atif continued, "Shakir had serious concerns about his daughter's future in a small town, especially given Pakistan's unstable political, socio-economic, and law-and-order conditions. He had asked the visitor to help him find a job for Mahnoor abroad."

"After the man's first visit, Shakir didn't hear from him for a few months. Then, last year, he showed up at the same hotel near Mohenjo-daro. This time, the visitor was alone. He gave Shakir an artifact from Mohenjo-daro and asked him to take an oath on his daughter's head. The oath stated that Shakir would not give the artifact to anyone except the person who would know his daughter's birth name. Shakir's daughter is not commonly known by the name Mahnoor; everyone calls her Marvi." Atif looked at Sarah while completing the translation. "Shakir realized that Sarah is the right person when he heard his daughter's birth name come from Sarah's mouth, which only his immediate family and the visitor knew."

Shakir did not wait for Atif to translate his message for rest of the group; he had already gone into the adjoining room. He returned shortly after Atif finished his translation, holding a bunch of keys. With difficulty, he opened the rusted lock on the box. There was an ancient-looking clay vase with a small neck.

Handing over the vase to Jennifer, Dave asked, "Do you think it's from Mohenjo-daro?"

Jennifer took the vase and inspected it. There were some aspects of the vase's design that resembled ones from the Indus Valley Civilization. However, the clay did not appear to be very old. She took a few minutes to inspect every corner of the vase and finally announced:

"No. This looks like a replica of an artifact from the Indus Valley Civilization."

"Should we just break it open?" Dave suggested. "There may be something inside."

"Okay, but let's do it carefully, to avoid damaging any clues inside." Jennifer, being an archeologist, always kept her key tools with her. She grabbed her handheld laser saw from the car and began working on the vase. In no time, she skillfully split it into two pieces.

"Another written note and a triangular gold coin," Dave said, looking at the contents of the vase. This time, the note was on a piece of paper and both items were wrapped in a thick plastic bag.

The third gold coin was similar in size and texture to the other two. However, the graphic inscription was different. This coin had symbols of moon and water engraved on its face.

Sarah read the note that accompanied this coin:

"Place the gold in perfect order to find the wonder that is rarely known."

Chapter 9

November 29 2:00 AM (PST)
Mohenjo-daro, Sindh, Pakistan

The group thanked Shakir for helping them and his daughter for her hospitality at this late hour.

As they were about to leave, Dave asked Atif, "Can you tell Shakir that as a token of appreciation, I will personally make sure that Mahnoor gets a job with one of my dad's companies in the USA?"

When Atif translated Dave's message, Shakir started crying with happiness. He placed his hand on top of Dave's head, giving him his blessings. He invited the group to stay in his home for the night, but Atif mentioned that he had made arrangements at a guesthouse near Mohenjo-daro.

The ride to the guesthouse was uneventful. Upon checking in, the group agreed to quickly freshen up and then meet in the common room to discuss the latest clue.

Atif had made reservations at this guesthouse after inquiring with the waiter at the restaurant in Naushahro Firoze. The waiter had wanted to warn him about a legend associated with this guesthouse, but Atif was happy to find any accommodation at that time and hadn't listened. It was common knowledge among the locals that the place was often visited by supernatural creatures. Called jinn, these beings were made of a smokeless, scorching fire and were believed to be possessors of celestial powers.

*****

The place was not fancy and had just the basic necessities like clean beds and washrooms. Within fifteen minutes of checking in, the group assembled in the large common room, which contained sofas, a television, and a pool table.

Dave began the conversation. "Where should we start?"

"Let's revisit all the clues," Sarah suggested.

Jennifer placed all the clues they had on a central table, and the group gathered around to inspect them.

The Lost Miracle

Clue#1: A note saying, 'Search for a lost civilization to unleash the road to a miraculous wonder that will change the face of earth,' and a triangular gold coin with symbols for 'Sun' and 'Sand' inscribed on it.

Clue#2: A note saying, 'The lost civilization is closer than you think,' and a triangular gold coin with a symbol for 'Fire' inscribed on it.

Clue#3: A note saying 'Place the gold in perfect order to find the wonder that is rarely known,' and a triangular gold coin with symbols for 'Moon' and 'Water' inscribed on it.

Analyzing the clues, Dave said, "Did you guys notice that, while the first clue introduced us to the miraculous wonder and guided us to Dubai, the coin was supposed to refer us to the shop named Sun and Sand in Dubai Mall. But we couldn't figure that out." He added, "Fortunately, Sarah's vision helped us get to the shop and find the second clue."

"Correct," said Jennifer, "and the note from the second clue directed us to the Indus Valley Civilization, while we could not pinpoint the logic for an inscription of fire." Then, Sarah's vision helped us yet again. We found Shakir, a firewood vendor, and the third clue. It is clear that the clues themselves are incomplete. There are some missing links."

Everyone looked at Sarah at the same time. This made her nervous, and she said, "I don't control my visions. They come on their own." She added in a defensive tone, "Don't look at me like that."

Jennifer came close to Sarah and wrapped her right hand around Sarah's shoulder. She said, "You are our savior. Without your help, we would not have been able to come this far."

Sarah gave an innocent smile.

Dave tried to get the conversation back on track. "Now, let's see what we have in the third clue," he said. "The note says that we need to place gold in perfect order to find a wonder that is rarely known."

Atif added his ten cents. "Gold means the triangle coins."

"Correct. Let's try to put the coins in all of the possible orders we can think of," Jennifer suggested.

Dave placed the coins in a row, like three mountains, but no one could make much sense from this order:

The Lost Miracle

Jennifer then stacked the three coins together, which also didn't make much sense:

All of them tried different options, one after another, but none of the options made sense.

Tony Agha

The Lost Miracle

Realizing that the whole team must be tired, Dave suggested, "Let's have a cup of coffee. We are all fatigued, and caffeine will provide a much-needed kick to our brains. Then, hopefully, we will be able to make some progress."

"Good idea!" said Jennifer and Atif at the same time. Atif called the guesthouse attendant and asked him to bring four strong cups of coffee.

Sarah took all three coins in her hand, hoping to connect with their aura, but she couldn't sense anything. She closed her eyes to concentrate and was surprised to feel the presence of someone other than Dave, Jennifer, and Atif. The vibrations she was feeling didn't appear to be coming from a human being. She tried to focus on these vibrations.

She felt a concentration of bright light in the center of the room. A figure began to form. It was something like a bright, translucent hologram. She could make out the figure's face, but its features were not clearly defined. It had two arms and a body similar to a man's; its legs, however, were like smoke. It was floating in the air.

Sarah opened her eyes. She was surprised to still see the figure in the room — normally, her visions went away when she returned to reality. With a gentle voice, Sarah looked in the direction of the mysterious being and asked, "Who are you?"

Tony Agha

Dave, Jennifer, and Atif were surprised at Sarah's question. They looked in the direction of her eyes but didn't see anything.

Jennifer started to say something, but Dave stopped her with a hand gesture.

The being looked at Sarah, apparently surprised to know that she could see him.

Sarah said, "My name is Sarah and these are my friends." She added, "We are all friends, so don't be afraid of us."

The being smiled, as if he was too strong to be scared of Sarah and her friends. He waved his right hand in front of himself from the bottom up and became visible to rest of the group.

Jennifer, Dave, and Atif looked at the creature with their mouths open wide. Their eyes looked like they had forgotten how to blink.

The being said something in a language that no one understood and pointed both his hands in the direction of the golden coins. Smoke came out of his hands and went to the coins, which started to float in thin air. After circling a couple of times, following each other, the coins arranged themselves in the shape of a pyramid. Keeping this shape, the coins descended back to the table.

The being said something else in the same language and disappeared, laughing loudly.

The Lost Miracle

It was difficult to say if the group was more shocked or excited: shocked at what they had just witnessed, but excited to see the coins in the following formation:

"What was that?" Jennifer said, finally finding her voice.

They all looked at Sarah, hoping to get some answers.

"Don't look at me, how should I know?" Sarah said, sounding surprised herself.

The group had not realized that the guesthouse attendant was also in the room. He had come in with their coffee and probably witnessed the event as well. He said something in the local language, which Atif apparently understood. Atif translated for the rest of them.

"This guy gave me his explanation of this episode." Atif continued, "He believes, like many other locals, that a group of jinn live close by and often wander around. However, he had never seen one before tonight."

"What do you mean?" Dave asked. "What are jinn?"

Atif replied, "According to our beliefs, jinn are supernatural creatures made of fire. They are possessors of celestial powers."

"Are they good or bad?" Dave asked.

"Like humans, some are good and some are evil," Atif responded.

"The way this jinni helped us, he surely looked good to me," Sarah said with a smile.

"True, we had not figured out this formation of the coins ourselves," Jennifer agreed.

"Anyway, it looks like our next destination is Egypt," Dave said, with excitement and a newfound energy in his voice.

Chapter 10

November 29 9:00 AM (PST)
Mohenjo-daro, Sindh, Pakistan

After sunrise, Jennifer announced that she could not leave without paying a visit to the Mohenjo-daro ruins after coming so close. Atif volunteered to drive her there. Dave, wanting to make some calls, hitched a ride with them to a nearby international calling facility. He did this because, somehow, all of their cellphones were blocked for international dialing.

Sarah was enjoying a quiet moment at the guesthouse with a cup of coffee and a cheese omelet. She had asked Dave to call her mother and tell her that she was safe and well so she wouldn't worry too much. As Sarah finished her coffee, Dave joined her at the table. He had just returned after hitching a ride with the guesthouse manager.

"I asked my agent to find the earliest flights to Egypt and to get our visas processed on an urgent basis," Dave told her.

Jennifer's voice came from behind them: "I don't think that this last clue meant Egypt." Sarah and Dave turned to see her entering the room with Atif. Before Dave could say anything, she continued, "Remember, the third note said to 'find the wonder that is rarely known.' When the jinni put the coins together in the pyramid formation, the signs of the sun and moon were on two sides."

"Yes, but why doesn't it relate to the pyramids in Egypt?" Dave said.

"Not many people know that there is a pyramid near Mexico City. In fact, there are two: the larger one is called the Pyramid of the Sun and the smaller one is called the Pyramid of the Moon," Jennifer explained. "They are also known as Teotihuacan, or the Mayan Pyramids."

"Oh, I see," Dave said, and echoed Jennifer's thoughts. "You mean to say that the signs depicting the sun and moon, combined with the note's mention of a wonder rarely known, is more appropriate to Mexico than to Egypt."

Sarah said, "I agree. Mexico sounds like a better option."

"Mexico it is then. I'll have to go quickly and call my travel agent," Dave said.

The Lost Miracle

Atif, who was speaking to someone over his cellphone, made a hand gesture asking Dave to hold off for a second. He spoke as soon as he finished his call. "I was speaking with Mr. Zaman. He is very concerned about your security and has arranged a chartered flight from Mohenjo-daro to Karachi."

Dave's eyes brightened at this. He said, "Wow, that is so kind of him. Please thank him on our behalf."

"Sure, I will do that," Atif replied with a smile. "I don't think there is a direct flight from Karachi to Mexico City."

"No worries, I'll ask my agent to get us a connection via Dubai," Dave replied. "I have to go there to pick up our luggage anyway."

*****

November 29 2:00 AM (GMT)
Approx. 9,000 miles away from Dubai, UAE

He was sitting in his large, leather chair in his elaborate office. The office was on the top floor of the headquarters of his business empire. After reading the report on his tablet, he looked up and addressed his most trusted associate.

"I am pleased with your team. They have been successful in following the subjects in Dubai and Pakistan without their knowledge."

"Thanks! I have hired the best of the best for this job," said the person sitting on the other side of the desk.

"So, you are saying that their next stop is Mexico?" asked the man in the leather chair.

"That is correct, and be assured that everything will go as per your plan in Mexico," his obedient deputy assured him.

The man smiled and waved the deputy away. He wanted to be left alone in his room.

*****

The Lost Miracle

November 29 4:30 PM (PST)
Mohenjo-daro Airport, Sindh, Pakistan

They were met by friendly staff at the Mohenjo-daro Airport, and their chartered airplane was waiting for them on the tarmac.

It took them less than fifteen minutes to board the plane, and another fifteen passed before takeoff.

"We should be in Karachi in thirty minutes," the pilot announced once they were in the air.

"Great! We will reach Karachi well before our 7:00 PM flight to Dubai," Dave exclaimed. "Finally, it appears that the tide has turned in our favor. Things are going as planned."

Dave's bliss was short lived. Ten minutes before the scheduled landing time, the pilot announced, "We have been denied permission to land at the Karachi international airport." He had a lot of concern in his voice. "A group of ten to fifteen terrorists has attacked the Quaid-e-Azam International Airport in Karachi with firearms and explosives. They are attempting to take control of the airport."

"Oh my God!" Jennifer exclaimed.

"The Civil Aviation Authority of Pakistan has closed all flight operations, and we will have to land at Nawabshah Airport," the pilot continued.

Dave immediately stood up and went to the pilot's cabin. He came back after ten minutes and said, "I explained our situation to the pilot and requested that he take us to Dubai instead of landing at Nawabshah." Dave continued, "The pilot is working on acquiring the authorizations."

"Did you ask the pilot to inform Mr. Zaman?" Atif asked Dave.

"Yes, the pilot will do that through the control tower. I have also told him that I will be bearing the expense for this detour," Dave responded. "We just can't take any more chances. The security situation is getting worse in Pakistan."

"I agree, it is not safe for us locals to stay here, let alone foreign nationals." Atif added with concern, "However, if we go to Dubai, I would be in a bit of a situation. I don't have my passport with me, and even if I had it, I don't have a visa to enter the UAE."

"We can deal with that when we get to Dubai. You shouldn't worry too much, I know some people at the UAE Foreign Ministry and Pakistani Consulate in Dubai," Dave said, and added, "Let's hope that the pilot gets permission from his bosses."

After circling the Karachi airport for thirty minutes, the pilot announced, "Congratulations, we have received permission to proceed to Dubai International Airport. We should be there in a couple of hours."

Dave, Jennifer, and Sarah sighed with relief. Atif was still concerned about his travel documents.

Their plane landed at Dubai International Airport, but they were not allowed to disembark until Atif's visa and passport issue had been resolved. It took around two hours and numerous calls for Dave to arrange a temporary travel document with a UAE visa for Atif.

*****

November 29 10:30 PM (GST)
Atlantis Hotel, Dubai, UAE

The group checked into the exotic Atlantis Hotel in Dubai. The Atlantis was a world-renowned hotel with an underwater theme park and fascinating restaurants. After a quick break, all four assembled in the Seafire Steakhouse & Bar, one of the hotel's landmark restaurants.

"What is their specialty?" Jennifer asked the waiter as she inspected the menu.

Dave gave his expert opinion. "The last time I visited, everything I tried was good. One thing that I highly recommend is their char-grilled jumbo tiger prawns. They are out of this world."

After the waiter had taken their order, Jennifer asked Dave, "Were you able to reserve our flight to Mexico City?"

"Yes, our flight will take off tomorrow at 11:00 AM GST. We will reach Mexico City at 7:30 PM CST the next day with a night layover at London Heathrow. I have also rented a car in Mexico."

"I hope that your plans work this time," Jennifer said sarcastically, showing her apprehension regarding Dave's planning skills.

Dave ignored Jennifer's sarcasm and changed the subject, directing a question to Atif. "I understand that the situation is still uncertain in Karachi. You are most welcome to stay here until things get sane there."

"Thanks!" Atif replied.

Realizing that she might not see Atif again, Jennifer got a little emotional. She placed her hand on Atif's and said, "We will miss you in Mexico. You stay safe in Karachi, and try to stay in touch."

Sarah and Dave looked at each other with surprised expressions. They had never seen Jennifer speaking in such a polite tone while showing her emotions for anyone before.

*****

Chapter 11

December 1 8:00 PM (CST)
Benito Juárez International Airport, Mexico City, Mexico

The first class seats of the British Airways flight to Mexico City were very comfortable. The trio was among the first to reach the immigration counter. The immigration officer didn't look very excited while inspecting their passports. After looking at the documents a couple of times, he pointed to another officer and said, "Can you please follow that lady to the secondary screening room?"

Dave, surprised by this request, said, "May I ask you the reason?"

The immigration officer didn't respond. He merely gestured to the person next in line.

They had no option but to oblige.

In the secondary screening room, they were asked to take a seat. The lady who had escorted them disappeared. They waited for an hour and a half in the room before another officer finally came in.

He said, "I apologize for keeping you waiting. Since you have visited Pakistan recently, we had to do some background checks." He handed them back their travel documents. "Welcome to Mexico!"

Jennifer thought that if they had to go through this as American citizens, what would Atif have to go through with his Pakistani passport?

After taking their luggage, they walked up to the rent-a-car office, which was within the airport terminal. The women decided to wait outside, letting Dave go into the office alone.

Dave came out after twenty minutes. He looked furious.

"What happened?" Jennifer asked.

"The smart ass gave my rental to someone else, thinking that we wouldn't show up," Dave replied.

"What the . . ." Jennifer kept herself from swearing and said, "So, are you saying that we don't have a car?"

"It's not that, we do have a car, but there is no GPS in the vehicle," Dave replied. "We can't use our phones because the cellular companies are on a strike. They have blocked the roaming facility for international subscribers."

"Can't we get a local SIM?" Sarah asked.

"No, I have already asked the guy." Dave shook his head. "No new connections until the government agrees to their terms."

"I guess we will have to go the old-fashioned way and use paper maps," Sarah said with a smile, trying to cool down Dave and Jennifer.

They searched the airport for a shop that sold road maps. Unfortunately, they could only find maps in Spanish.

Jennifer suggested, "Let's buy it. Something is better than nothing."

It took them some time, but the trio was able to jot down the route to their hotel on the map. Dave took the steering wheel, and Jennifer was again the designated co-pilot.

Sarah commented on their rental, a black Volkswagen Jetta with a 2.4 liter engine. "Well, at least we got a nice car," she said, trying yet again to change her friends' moods.

"Yes, the car is sexy, unlike Dave's sunglasses," Jennifer said, making fun of Dave's unconventional sunglasses.

"I like them, and that's all that matters to me," Dave said sarcastically. "Can you please concentrate on the map and tell me where to turn?"

"What is there to concentrate on?" Jennifer mumbled. "I wish I had taken my Spanish classes in school seriously."

The Lost Miracle

"Oh, shoot, we will have to take a detour," Dave said, noticing some construction occurring on the main road. He turned the car toward an inner street.

"I don't think this street is on the map," Jennifer commented, trying to follow their twists and turns on the paper.

As Jennifer was trying to figure out a way to get them back onto Main Street, a big truck appeared at their side. In a rash maneuver, it pulled in front of them, cutting their vehicle off. Shortly after, another truck approached them from behind. The trucks almost squeezed their car by driving too close, forcing them to stop.

Four masked men emerged from the trucks and ordered them to close their eyes. They felt their hands being tied and their eyes blindfolded. The captors moved Dave and Jennifer to the back seat of the Jetta and took over the driver's seat.

"Who are you, and what do you want?" Dave asked the person driving their car, but he didn't get an answer.

After around thirty minutes of driving, the car stopped. They were forcibly removed from the car and led into a building. Upon entering the building, their captors removed their blindfolds. One of the kidnappers, who appeared to be the leader of the group, picked up his phone and made a call. He spoke to the person on the other side in what sounded like Spanish.

The building looked like an abandoned shed of an old warehouse that had not been used for quite some time. There were spider webs in every corner, thick layers of dust on floor, and rusted metal furniture.

As the chief captor finished his call, he said, "Sí señor, comprendo," and all four kidnapers left the room.

"Are they going to kill us?" Jennifer asked fearfully.

"I don't know," Dave replied. "But I know that they are taking instructions from someone. The guy said 'Sí señor, comprendo,' which means 'Yes sir, I understand' in English."

Ignoring Dave's assessment, Jennifer said, "I don't want to die now."

Sarah tried to comfort her. "You will not die here," she said. "Trust me."

At that moment, they heard loud gunshots. After a few minutes, six men dressed in some kind of security service uniform barged in. The guards untied their ropes, then one of them said in a low voice, "Don't be scared. We are here to save you. Follow us quickly and keep low. We are not out of danger yet."

The trio obliged and followed the guards. As they sneaked out, they saw two Dodge Ram trucks parked outside the building. The drivers were waiting in the trucks with the engines turned on idle. The guards and freed captives got into the trucks and sped away.

"Who are you? Where are we going, and how did you know we were being kidnapped?" Dave asked in a single breath.

"You will get your answers soon," one of the guards responded.

*****

Chapter 12

December 1 11:00 PM (CST)
Mexico City, Mexico

After more than an hour of driving, the trucks approached a charming and elegant slate-roofed, ivy-covered mansion with beautifully landscaped lawns spread over ten acres of land. Large iron gates greeted them upon entering the estate, which opened onto a bucolic, tree-lined driveway.

The guards parked the trucks inside a large motor court. They were ushered into the mansion, entering through the main, large wooden gate toward the dining room. The mansion was huge. From inside, it encompassed more than 12,000 square feet of living space with ten bedrooms and twelve bathrooms. There was a foyer with a limestone staircase, and the main living room was formally decorated with a beamed ceiling and French doors.

The Lost Miracle

The dining room was also very formal, with French doors, a gourmet kitchen with rustic stone walls, and a conservatory with a fireplace. They walked through an entertaining terrace and a wood paneled library. They arrived in the dining room, where a large window overlooked stunning, park-like grounds that had a lavish swimming pool with a pool house, a lake, and a tennis court.

They were greeted by a very well-dressed man in his early sixties, who was seated in the most elegant chair at the dining table. A grand, four-course dinner of Mexican cuisine was awaiting them.

The gentleman had medium-length grey hair with light curls. Leaving the pipe that he was smoking in his mouth, he made a couple of hand gestures, ordering the guards to leave and offering the visitors a seat.

"I am Marcus," said their host. "You must be wondering why you are here."

"Yes, and do you mind explaining what is going on?" Jennifer asked. She was sounding upset and confused at recent events.

Sarah stared at Jennifer, silently urging her to soften her tone.

"It is late," Marcus said, ignoring Jennifer's sarcasm. "I know you must be hungry. Please, have something to eat as we speak." Taking a sip from his soup, he said, "I am an old friend of your father, Dave."

"Have we met before?" Dave asked.

Marcus answered, "No, I rarely go to the US. Your father and I meet outside of the states, mostly at international conferences in South America and Europe."

"But how did you know we were coming to Mexico City?" Dave asked.

"Your father called me while you were en route to Mexico City from Dubai," Marcus clarified. "He was a bit concerned after what you had to go through in Pakistan. He had asked me to keep an eye on you without informing you."

"That's right. I told Dad that we preferred to be left alone during our stay in Mexico," Dave confirmed.

"How did your guys find us when we got kidnapped?" Jennifer asked. Her tone was much softer this time.

"One of my staff members followed you from the airport," Marcus said. "When the group of assailants kidnapped you, he informed me, and I sent my guards to that location to retrieve you."

"Does that mean you don't know who our kidnappers were or what their objective was?" Sarah asked.

"Correct. I was about to ask you that question," Marcus responded. "In any case, may I ask the purpose of your visit to Mexico?"

The Lost Miracle

"We came . . ." Jennifer began. She was cut short by Dave, who placed his hand on her shoulder and said:

"We are here to visit the 'Basilica de Nuestra Señora de Guadalupe' and participate in the annual celebration of Our Lady of Guadalupe's feast day."

Jennifer and Sarah looked at Dave in surprise.

Sarah knew about the Basilica de Nuestra Señora de Guadalupe very well, as it was regarded as one of the holiest sites of Catholicism in America. She recalled her mother telling her about the church at a young age. It was built near a place where a Native American named Juan Diego claimed to have seen a vision of 'Our Lady of Guadalupe' in a blue mantle in 1531. 'Our Lady of Guadalupe,' also known as the 'Virgin of Guadalupe,' was a title of the Virgin Mary associated with a celebrated pictorial image housed in the Basilica of Our Lady of Guadalupe in Mexico City.

"You are a bit early for the feast day. It is on December 12," Marcus replied. After thinking for a few seconds, he continued. "Considering your welcome party this evening, I think it is not safe for you to stay in Mexico City for that long. I suggest that you return home as soon as possible."

"We have come all this way and wouldn't want to leave without visiting." Dave sounded determined.

"Very well. In that case, I urge you to stay within my estate as much as possible. If you have to go out, my guards will accompany you."

Dave didn't complain.

At this point, a butler entered the room and announced, "The guest rooms have been prepared. Please call me when you are ready to retire for the night, and I will be happy to escort you to your accommodation."

"I am done and super tired," Sarah said

"Me, too," Jennifer echoed.

"Sure, I understand. I'll see you at breakfast." Marcus excused them from the table.

All three were provided exquisite bedrooms with elaborate bathrooms. They took relaxing baths and then changed into fresh clothing, which was also provided by their host since they had lost their luggage during the kidnapping.

Chapter 13

December 2 9:30 AM (CST)
Marcus' Estate, Near Mexico City, Mexico

Sarah and Jennifer arrived together at the breakfast table that was set up for them at the pool house. The table was only set for two. Seeing the surprised look on their faces, the butler informed them, "Mr. Marcus and your friend have already had breakfast."

"Where are they now?" asked Sarah.

"Mr. Marcus left for his office and your friend stepped out for a walk around the estate," the butler replied.

"That's strange, I have never seen Dave wake up so early before," Sarah commented.

After a few minutes, they saw Dave walking toward them, accompanied by two armed guards. He was smartly dressed in a black twill blazer with a steel grey t-shirt and black jeans.

"Nice clothes, Dave," Jennifer commented, with a touch of cynicism. "I would have said you are looking good, but your funny sunglasses are making it difficult."

Dave replied, "All I can say is that you need to upgrade your taste in men's fashion."

"You got up very early. Did you sleep well?" Sarah asked Dave, concerned.

"Yes, I'm good. Can you guys hurry up with your breakfast? We need to leave soon," Dave replied.

"Where are we going?" Jennifer asked.

"We are going to the Basilica de Nuestra Señora de Guadalupe," Dave responded, looking at the two guards who were standing beside him. "I have spoken with Marcus. He is okay if we take these two gentlemen with us."

"Basilica de Nuestra Señora de Guadalupe?" Jennifer and Sarah spoke at the same time with puzzled looks. Their original plan had been to go to the pyramids.

"Come on, move it now. We can talk when we get there," Dave said, avoiding the topic.

Traffic was heavy, and the trip to the Basilica took them a good hour and a half. During this long commute, Sarah provided a brief background of the Basilica de Nuestra Señora de Guadalupe to Jennifer, who, being a non-religious person, rarely remembered details about religious practices.

The Lost Miracle

Sarah explained, "According to tradition, an image of the Virgin Mary appeared on the tilma of Juan Diego. The image is preserved in the Basilica of Our Lady of Guadalupe, which attracts millions of pilgrims annually."

Upon reaching the Roman Catholic Church, Dave informed the guards, "We need to go inside the new Basilica. Since firearms cannot be taken in there, I suggest that you guys stay here."

Reluctantly, the guards obliged.

The trio commenced their walk toward the new Basilica, a circular structure next to the historic old Basilica. The original image of the Virgin of Guadalupe was now housed in this new Basilica.

In the long line of people, Dave overheard a group of American tourists talking with each other. They were planning to go to the pyramids right after visiting the Basilica.

Dave used his charm to hitch a ride with this group, and the trio managed to sneak out of the Basilica from a lesser-used door, avoiding the main exit where the guards were waiting for them.

*****

It took them a little under an hour to reach the pyramids from the Basilica. During the ride, the group's tour guide gave an overview of the Teotihuacán Pyramids. She explained:

"Tall and mysterious, the Pyramids of the Sun and Moon rise above silent Teotihuacán, an empty city that once bustled with as many as 200,000 people and stood at the center of Mexico's pre-Hispanic empire." The guide continued, "They were erected by a virtually unknown culture in the first century B.C. The city sprawled over an area larger than imperial Rome. But by 750 A.D., it had been abruptly abandoned, perhaps because of a disaster or drought."

"Oh, really? I thought the Aztecs built them," said someone from the tour group.

"Actually, it was around five hundred years later when the Aztecs came upon the pre-Columbian Mesoamerican city of Teotihuacán." The guide elaborated with pride of knowledge evident on her face, "Fascinated with its pyramids, temples, apartments, and ball courts, the Aztecs adopted it as a center of pilgrimage."

"Are these pyramids as high as the pyramids in Egypt?" another person asked.

"Good question," the guide replied with a smile. "The Pyramid of the Sun is roughly 210 feet high and ranks as one of the largest pyramids in the world. However, it is about half as tall as the Great Pyramid of Giza in Egypt."

The Lost Miracle

"The builders raised the Pyramid of the Sun around 100 A.D., somehow transporting and erecting three million tons of stone, brick, and rubble without the benefits of the wheel, beasts of burden, or metal tools. After climbing 248 steps to the top of the pyramid, you can survey the temple-lined Avenue of the Dead, a roadway about two-and-a-half miles long that ends with the Pyramid of the Moon rising to the north. That pyramid was completed before 300 A.D."

The guide looked at the person who had previously inquired about the height and said with a smile, "I am sure you must be wondering: the Pyramid of the Moon, although it appears to be as tall as the Pyramid of the Sun, is only 150 feet tall, but is built on higher ground."

The tour guide didn't mention an interesting fact that Jennifer knew well. In 1971, archaeologists had found a previously unknown entryway some 320 feet long that led to a cave directly beneath the apex of the pyramid.

At one time, the cave had held a natural spring, and there were still piles of charcoal in the chamber. This, perhaps, indicated ceremonies involving water and fire. No one knew for sure, and the mystery of what really happened there persisted.

The pyramids were crowded by tourists. The trio thanked the tour group for giving them a ride and parted ways to carry on with their own expedition.

Dave looked at Sarah and Jennifer and said, "How about we start with a survey of the place and try to identify any link to the signs we've found so far?"

"The Avenue of the Dead is the central pathway that connects the Pyramid of the Sun and the Pyramid of the Moon," said Jennifer. She suggested, "Let's start with the Pyramid of Sun."

The trio walked along the Avenue of the Dead and climbed the stairs of the two pyramids, but couldn't find anything that grabbed their attention.

"What, exactly, are we looking for?" Sarah asked after the trio had surveyed the city a couple of times.

"We have symbols of sun and sand, fire and moon, and water," Jennifer replied, recalling the clues they had so far. "Try to find something that is linked to these symbols individually or on a holistic level."

Dave asked Sarah, "Have you seen any visions lately?"

Sarah shook her head.

Jennifer said, "Let's walk toward the market compound and find something to eat, or at least drink, before we faint of malnutrit . . ."

Before she could complete her sentence, they heard someone calling their names. They looked back and noticed that the tour guide from the tourist group was shouting their names and waving to them.

"We are going to a nearby restaurant," she said. "Would you like to join us?"

The Lost Miracle

The trio was starving and could not refuse the offer. They waved back at the friendly tour guide and walked toward the group.

*****

The tour bus stopped at the La Gruta restaurant, which was 0.4 miles from the pyramids. The restaurant was built into a real cave, beautifully decorated in traditional Mexican style.

The group dispersed, and families, friends, and couples took separate tables. Dave, Sarah, and Jennifer found a nice table far from the stage, on which a group was performing live music. The musicians were dressed in traditional attire and were performing catchy Spanish songs.

After the usher gave them menus and left, Sarah announced, "I need to go to the ladies' room." Handing over her menu to Jennifer, she asked, "Can you order for me whatever you are getting for yourself?"

The restroom was empty when Sarah entered it. She opened the tap and mixed the water until it was the right temperature for her. Sarah closed her eyes and splashed a handful of water on her face. She opened her eyes and looked toward the mirror. Instead of her own reflection, she saw, with her eyes open, a vision.

It was a desert-like place with brown sand all over and little vegetation. There was a small town that appeared to be from an ancient era. A person who was thought to be dead was found alive. The whole town gathered around that person's house with surprised looks on their faces.

Nearby, a large number of toy-sized bicycles were attached to iron rods in multiple rows, like some sort of old-fashioned assembly line.

She heard a voice: "Are you okay . . . are you okay?"

Startled, Sarah came back to reality. A young girl was looking at her in amazement and asking her if she

The Lost Miracle

was okay. She quickly washed her face and walked back to her table to join Dave and Jennifer.

"You are just in time," Jennifer said, pointing toward the fresh appetizers on the table.

"I just had another vision," Sarah announced, and described the vision to Dave and Jennifer.

"I am unable to derive any meaning from your vision, Sarah," Dave said. He leaned back in his chair, deep in thought, trying to interpret the bizarre imagery.

"So am I," Sarah replied, and took a cheese-dipped nacho from the appetizer platter.

At that moment, the musicians stopped playing their tunes. They seemed to be taking a break.

The sounds of music were now replaced by the voices of people conversing at their respective tables.

A particular conversation going on at an adjacent table caught their attention. An elderly lady was talking to a couple of young kids who appeared to be her grandchildren.

"Hurry up and finish your food. We have to get back to the souvenir shop as soon as possible," she said excitedly.

"What happened, Grandma?" one of the kids asked.

"Your father is alive. Someone found him unconscious and brought him back to the souvenir shop when he woke up."

The kids' faces lit up with joy.

Sarah couldn't stop herself. She turned back to speak with the elderly lady. "I am sorry, but I overheard your conversation. If you don't mind my asking, is everything okay?"

"Yes, all is well now," the elderly lady replied with a smile. She shared her story. "We are from London, England, on holiday here in Mexico. We were shopping for souvenirs this morning when my son went out for a walk. He didn't return, and had been missing for three hours."

She moved closer to Sarah and continued. "We searched everywhere but couldn't find any sign of him. We thought that we had lost him, but fortunately he has returned now, well and alive."

"That's great!" Sarah told her. After a pause, she said to the lady, "Can I ask you for a favor?"

"Sure, what can I do for you?" the lady replied.

"We are also tourists, and we were hoping to go to a souvenir shop. Can you give us a ride?" Sarah asked.

"I am sorry my dear, but I don't have a car," the British lady replied. She pointed to a Mexican family sitting at a nearby table. "We came with that family. They were at the shop when this happened and were very kind. They stayed with us throughout. They were concerned for my grandchildren and volunteered to drive us here, so the kids could eat something."

The Lost Miracle

Sarah turned back to Dave and Jennifer. Before Sarah could open her mouth, Jennifer said, "I know, we need to go to that souvenir shop."

"I agree," said Dave. "Your vision also featured a person coming back after being presumed dead. We should find a lead there."

Chapter 14

December 2 4:30 PM (CST)
Souvenir Shop, San Juan Teotihuacán, Mexico

Dave used his charm to convince the Mexican family to give them a ride to the souvenir shop. Fortunately, they drove a big van that was able to fit all of them.

The souvenir shop was decorated in the traditional Mexican style. The trio didn't find anything relevant in the shop. As a courtesy, they briefly spoke with the young man who had gone missing.

After hearing the man's story and inspecting the shop from all angles a few times, Sarah said, "Let's ask the girl at counter if there is a souvenir factory nearby that manufactures small cycles."

"Good idea!" Dave said, and approached the cute Mexican girl at the counter.

The Lost Miracle

"Hi! You have very unique souvenirs in your shop. May I ask where you buy them?" Dave asked the girl.

The beautiful teenager responded with pride, "We have our own factory, five minutes' walk from here."

"Wow! Do they also manufacture bicycles?" Dave asked.

The girl thought for a second and replied. "I am not sure what they are producing right now. Every few days, they make bulk quantities of different products that are sold here at the shop and distributed across Mexico."

The trio easily located the factory with the directions the shop attendant gave them. The main door was locked. They walked around the factory in the hope of finding another entrance.

"Hey, look. There's a window. Dave, you're the tallest, can you try and peek inside?" Jennifer asked. "If you see anyone, try and grab his attention."

Dave found a wooden box and stepped up on it to peek inside. Upon looking in, he said, "Oh my God. Sarah, you need to come and see this for yourself."

Dave lifted Sarah over his shoulders so she could look inside. Sarah was excited to see fifteen to twenty long iron rods, each with small bicycles attached. Each rod held around ten bicycles.

As Sarah was peeking inside from the high window, she heard a man shouting, "Qué deseas?"

Fortunately, the shopkeeper had given them the name of the factory owner. Dave, not completely understanding what the man was saying, replied with the owner's name: "Roberto."

The man, apparently a security guard taking his routine round outside the perimeter of the factory, said "Sígueme," and began walking.

The trio didn't quite understand what he meant, but assumed that he wanted them to follow him and did so.

The factory guard took them to another small shed nearby, which appeared to be the factory's office. He directed them to a heavyset young man with a long, Mexican-style moustache.

"Hi, are you Roberto?" Dave asked him.

"Yes. How can I help you?" Roberto replied with a heavy Spanish accent.

Dave gave him as much background detail as the situation required. When he finished, he asked Roberto if he had something to give them.

To their surprise, Roberto answered, "Are you Mr. Solomon's son?"

Startled to hear his father's name, Dave replied, "Yes, how do you know?"

"I was actually expecting your father," Roberto said. He walked toward his office cabinets.

"My good friend, Robert, gave me a picture of your father and said he would come to collect this,"

The Lost Miracle

Roberto added, searching the cabinet for something. "You look at lot like your father."

Roberto finally found what he was looking for. He turned back to them and placed it on the table in front of them.

It was a bottle of tequila.

Surprised, Jennifer replied, "Oh, thank you for your hospitality, but we would appreciate it if you could give us the thing that Rob left for us."

Roberto looked at Jennifer as if she had asked a very stupid question. He pointed toward the center of the bottle, urging them to look inside.

"Oh my God!" Jennifer gasped when she looked where he pointed. There was a small glass ball inside the tequila bottle.

"Can we break the bottle?" Dave asked.

Roberto smiled and gave him a glass cutting saw.

Dave emptied the liquid into another bottle and started gently cutting the bottle. The glass ball inside the bottle was actually two half spheres joined together.

Dave twisted the two parts to open the glass ball. There was a tightly sealed plastic bag holding another triangular gold coin and a folded piece of paper. He quickly took the coin and paper out of the plastic bag.

"This looks like a symbol for air," Jennifer said, looking at the inscription on this fourth triangle.

Tony Agha

Dave unfolded the piece of paper and placed it on a nearby table.

Sarah and Jennifer came closer to see what was written on the paper.

"This appears to be incomplete. There is a big blank spot in the middle," Jennifer said, looking at the paper.

Sarah analyzed the piece of paper. There were four small symbols of fire, earth, wind, and water. She thought for a minute and said, "Wait a minute. I think I know how to get the missing text." She took the other three coins out of her pocket and grabbed the fourth one from Jennifer's hands. She placed them upside-down on the paper with the top point of each triangle touching the others in a flower-like sequence:

The Lost Miracle

She matched the symbols of fire, earth, wind, and water on the paper with the respective symbol on each coin.

There were lines on the back side of each coin that didn't make sense individually, but when placed on the paper in this sequence revealed an inscription.

"Wow! This looks like some sort of process diagram and a formula," Dave exclaimed.

They heard a familiar voice say, "Well done!" Everyone turned in the direction of the voice. Marcus was standing in the doorway with his two guards.

"Can I see the formula?" Marcus asked politely, and started walking toward them.

Dave looked around and noticed that there was a bottle labeled 'aqua regia' close to him. He recalled his old chemistry professor telling them that aqua regia was a highly corrosive acid that can dissolve gold very quickly. He swiftly dropped all four coins into the acid and ate the piece of paper.

Marcus couldn't believe what he was witnessing. The gold coins started to dissolve in the liquid. Even if he tried to get them out from the glass bottle it was too late; the markings on the coins would have been destroyed by now.

"What the . . ." Marcus shouted, surprised by Dave's actions.

"Rob lost his life saving this formula," Dave said. "If the world can't have it, neither can you."

"You have really upset me now, and I have no other option but to kill you." Marcus was steaming with anger.

Sarah and Jennifer looked at Dave and Marcus in confusion. They weren't expecting this behavior from either of them. A number of questions bombarded their brains: why had Dave destroyed the coins and the formula after traveling across the globe to search for them? Why was Marcus willing to kill them for this formula, and how did he know about it? How had he found them? And, most importantly of all, what was this formula?

Some of their questions were quickly answered by Marcus, who spoke furiously.

"Do you have any idea of the damage you've done?" he shouted at Dave.

The Lost Miracle

"When Rob stumbled over that formula, I thought I could fulfill my dream of becoming the richest person on Earth." Marcus had moved beyond anger now, and there was remorse in his voice. "He didn't own the formula. It was a lucky break for him when lightning struck his experiment and this wonderful miracle was discovered."

Sarah and Jennifer were looking at both Marcus and Dave in confusion, their eyes wide, trying to figure out what was going on.

"I tried persuading, bribing, and threatening Rob," Marcus continued, his eyes again red with rage. "But he wanted to share it with the world. He wanted to change the world and the fate of the common man."

"I told him that we could make billions regulating the use of it . . . but it's too late now," Marcus said. He looked unable to control his anger.

"All of you stand in line; I want to finish this quickly," he ordered Dave, Sarah, Jennifer, and Roberto.

"Before you pull the trigger, please at least tell us what is going on. What is this formula?" Jennifer said, sounding fearful.

Marcus thought for a minute and then said "Rob, as Dave knows well, was a scientist. His expertise was in the petrochemicals industry. We were good friends. Last year, with the help of a miracle, Rob discovered an extremely low-cost compound that had amazing properties when processed in a particular way."

"Rob discovered it when lightning struck his experiment." After a long pause, Marcus continued. "When Rob added a few drops of his compound to purified gasoline, after the gasoline had passed through sand with a high electrostatic discharge, a miracle happened."

"What kind of miracle?" Jennifer asked with curiosity.

Marcus looked at Dave like he was about to break his bones. He said, "The process increases the efficiency of gasoline by twenty times. This means that the amount you used to pay for gas in one month would now be good for two years." Sighing deeply, Marcus continued. "Rob shared his findings with me and asked me if I could fund its production on a mass scale. He wanted to share the low cost benefits with the world, but I had other plans. I wanted to release the product wisely and make stupendous profits. He would be alive if he had listened to me."

"How did you know that we were searching for this miracle?" Jennifer asked, stunned at the information she had just received.

Marcus responded, now looking lost and defeated. "When Rob found out that I wanted to steal his formula, he went underground." He took a few seconds to take a cigar out of his pocket and light it before continuing. "We were able to track him to a cottage in Muskoka, but unfortunately, before I could get the formula from him, he committed suicide."

Marcus took a couple of deep puffs of his expensive Cuban cigar and spoke again. "My contacts informed me that Rob had sent a parcel to Dave's father. Seeing a ray of hope, I assigned a team of private agents to follow his every move. After months of fruitless sleuthing, we got excited again when Dave made extensive inquiries about an ancient wooden chest shortly after his father had visited him. I switched my attention to Dave and instructed my team to follow his every move and trace his calls."

Even with that rage burning inside, a faint smile touched Marcus' face. He said, "I increased my surveillance of Dave when he reached Dubai, as according to my intel, Rob had also visited that city shortly before he died." Marcus settled himself on a nearby chair and continued. "My team gave me detailed reports every hour of your activities in Dubai and Pakistan. When I found out about your plans to come to Mexico City, I also flew here."

"Oh, I get it," Jennifer said, sounding as if things were becoming clear. "So you're the one who kidnapped us. Then you pretended to save us to gain our trust so that we would give you the formula when we found it."

Marcus gave an evil smile but said nothing.

"One last question," Jennifer asked. "How did you find us here?"

Marcus shouted back, "Enough with your questions." He extinguished his cigar on a nearby table and pointed his gun at Dave. He said, "It is time to die now."

As Marcus was about to pull the trigger, they heard a shot. The gun fell out of Marcus' hand. Within a split second, five policemen barged into the room and grabbed Marcus and his guards. They were followed by a middle-aged man in plain clothes, who entered the room after the situation was under control.

Dave smiled, hugged the plain-clothed man, and said:

"You have no idea how glad I am to see you, Uncle Carlos."

"Can someone explain to me what is going on?" Jennifer shouted, looking at Dave.

"Sarah and Jen, meet my father's close friend, Uncle Carlos," Dave said, and explained, "I started doubting Marcus when he introduced himself as Dad's friend. I know Uncle Carlos very well, and if my dad had asked anyone to help us, it would have been Uncle Carlos."

"Come on, let's get out of here. We can talk in the car," Carlos said.

As they left the room, Dave continued with his explanation. "At the mansion, I found an open Wi-fi

The Lost Miracle

connection and sent a message to my dad with our plan to go to the pyramids."

"I'll tell you what happened after that," Carlos interrupted.

They got into Carlos' car. As he started the engine, Carlos said, "Dave's father called and told me the whole story." He continued, "I went straight to the policía, and we traced you to the factory through the people you talked to at the pyramids, the restaurant, and the shop."

"But how did you send the message, Dave?" Jennifer asked. "You don't have a computer, and our phones were snatched when we got kidnapped in Mexico City."

Dave smiled and said, "Here, check out my glasses." He handed the glasses over to Jennifer and explained, "These are the latest, not yet released version of state-of-the-art computer glasses. They've got a high-definition optical display, Wi-fi connectivity, and built-in memory."

Jennifer put the glasses on and was amazed to see information displayed in them. It was better than a smartphone's hands-free format. She asked, "How do you enter information without a keyboard?"

Dave replied, "It has an option to communicate with the Internet via voice commands."

"Wait a minute — so the miracle isn't lost!" Jennifer exclaimed with joy, looking through the glasses with their high-tech screen. "You took a picture of the process with the formula and saved it on this device."

Dave smiled.

Epilogue

December 20
Montvale, NJ, USA

Dave flew to New Jersey to visit Sarah and Jennifer in Montvale before heading off to spend the Christmas holidays with his family. They were chilling out at the indoor swimming pool in Sarah's backyard.

"It's good that you could drop by. We never really had a chance to relax and catch up during our adventure," Sarah said, handing some snacks over to Dave.

"Yeah, it's like old times," Jennifer said. "But since you have touched on the topic, I still don't get how Marcus found us at the factory."

"That's easy," Sarah said. "His guards must have inquired at the Basilica and found out that we had left with a tour group for the pyramids. From there, they could have traced us to the factory via the restaurant and the souvenir shop. Same way Carlos found us."

Dave changed the subject. "By the way, remember how I told you that I shared the formula with the State Department?" Sarah and Jennifer nodded. Jennifer asked, "Yes, what did they say?"

"They were able to recreate and test the process and formula, and they were amazed to see that it really works," Dave said excitedly. "The department also assured us that they will be rolling it out on the market at a very low cost, so that common people can reap its benefits."

"That is amazing!" Sarah exclaimed. "Now Rob's dream will come true, and this miracle will change the face of the planet for coming generations."

References

- Multiple references see article "Indus Valley Civilization" – http://en.wikipedia.org/wiki/Indus_Valley_Civilization

- Multiple references see article "Mohenjo-daro" – http://en.wikipedia.org/wiki/Mohenjo-daro

- Multiple references see article "Teotihuacan" – http://en.wikipedia.org/wiki/Teotihuacan

- Dunn, Jr, Jerry Camarillo. "Pyramids of the Sun and Moon at Teotihuacan" May 25, 2007. HowStuffWorks.com. <http://adventure.howstuffworks.com/pyramids-of-the-sun-and-moon-at-teotihuacan-landmark.htm> July 2, 2014.

- Department of AAOA. "Teotihuacan: Pyramids of the Sun and the Moon." In *Heilbrunn Timeline of Art History*. New York: The Metropolitan Museum of Art, 2000–. http://www.metmuseum.org/toah/hd/teot2/hd_teot2.htm (October 2001)

Tony Agha travelled to far-flung corners of the earth and came into contact with many distinct cultures. These experiences surfaced in his fiction when Tony embarked on his career as an author. Many of the characters and situations in his stories are derived from the author's own experiences, although heightened through his imagination. This brings a grounding of reality to all his work by enabling the reader to establish an immediate connection with the protagonists he creates.

Connect with the author at:
facebook.com/AuthorTonyAgha
twitter: @AuthorTonyAgha
email: Tony.Agha@MythShack.com

ISBN 978-0-9938656-0-2

Made in the USA
Charleston, SC
30 July 2014